"Then I guess yo
her hand in Dallas

"And vice-versa." He led her to the dance floor and drew her expertly into his arms. "But just to be clear — if there were a hundred single women in this room, I'd still rather dance with you."

Her heart did a stutter-step. If he'd agreed to back off, he shouldn't be saying things like that. "Because I'm good at it?"

"That's one reason." He tightened his grip on her waist and executed a fancy spin.

"Too bad I'm so young." Being a smartass was her only defense. Close contact with his virile body robbed her of breath and sent her pulse into overdrive.

"Too bad I'm so old." He twirled her around again.

She gulped for air. "At least you're spry for your age." He wasn't even breathing fast, the rat.

"I stay active." He flashed her a grin. "Having fun, yet?"

Oh, yeah. Way too much fun.

TEMPTING THE COWBOY'S SISTER

ROWDY RANCH

Vicki Lewis Thompson

Ocean Dance Press

TEMPTING THE COWBOY'S SISTER
© 2023 Vicki Lewis Thompson

ISBN: 978-1-63803-937-2

Ocean Dance Press LLC
PO Box 69901
Oro Valley, AZ 85737

Visit the author's website at
VickiLewisThompson.com

Want more cowboys? Check out these other titles by
Vicki Lewis Thompson

Rowdy Ranch
Having the Cowboy's Baby
Stoking the Cowboy's Fire
Testing the Cowboy's Resolve
Rocking the Cowboy's Christmas
Roping the Cowboy's Heart
Tempting the Cowboy's Sister

The Buckskin Brotherhood
Sweet-Talking Cowboy
Big-Hearted Cowboy
Baby-Daddy Cowboy
True-Blue Cowboy
Strong-Willed Cowboy
Secret-Santa Cowboy
Stand-Up Cowboy
Single-Dad Cowboy
Marriage-Minded Cowboy
Gift-Giving Cowboy

The McGavin Brothers
A Cowboy's Strength
A Cowboy's Honor
A Cowboy's Return
A Cowboy's Heart
A Cowboy's Courage
A Cowboy's Christmas
A Cowboy's Kiss
A Cowboy's Luck
A Cowboy's Charm
A Cowboy's Challenge

1

Dallas Armstrong had found his place in life. His job as a firefighter for Wagon Train Fire and Rescue suited him right down to the ground. The dedication of the crew, the camaraderie at the station and the appreciation of the townspeople hit all the right notes. Chief Denny Portman was a natural leader.

His shift at the firehouse ended at eight in the morning. He was usually tuckered out by the time he drove back to Rowdy Ranch and this May morning was no exception.

But it was a good kind of tired. Working side-by-side with folks he liked and respected was rewarding. That said, he looked forward to four days off so he could putter around his log cabin.

Technically it wasn't *his* cabin. Yet. He'd rented it a year ago from fellow firefighter, Cheyenne McLintock. Cheyenne likely wouldn't ever live in it again now that he'd settled into wedded bliss at Kendall's place on a small neighboring spread. Eventually Dallas would have enough put by to make an offer.

He'd be closer to that goal if he hadn't bought a horse. But Angie, Cheyenne's younger sister, had insisted a cowboy needed a horse. Soon after her birthday in February, she'd dragged him to a neighboring ranch to see the one she'd found for him. He'd fallen in love with the dappled gray.

Angie had piled on reasons to take the gelding home — the bargain price with saddle included, free boarding in the McLintock's barn, brothers who would give him the family rate for shoeing and vet fees, plus he'd get discounts on hay and grain because the ranch bought in bulk.

But he wasn't stupid. It would add up and cut into the savings plan he hadn't told anyone about. Then Angie had proposed changing the horse's name from Spotty, which they both detested, to Smoky, perfect for a firefighter's horse.

Resistance had been futile, especially when Angie had given him the luminous blue-eyed gaze that melted his heart and warmed up the rest of him pretty good, too.

That was another fact he couldn't reveal to anyone, least of all Angie. He was crazy about her. Who wouldn't be, especially after a year of getting to know her?

She'd taken little notice of him, though, so he'd stuffed his feelings. Then on her birthday, as if some switch had been flicked, she'd treated him like the best thing since sliced pumpernickel. A couple of days later she'd talked him into buying a horse and suggested they could go riding together.

Her about-face had made him happy but cautious. Good thing, because he'd no sooner moved Smoky into the barn than Cheyenne had paid him a visit.

According to Cheyenne, Angie's previous romances had been short-lived and superficial. Could be because she was young, only twenty-five. He'd mentioned it several times.

Message received. Evidently it didn't matter that Kendall had been the same age when their romance bloomed. Cheyenne and his brothers weren't keen on a thirty-two-year-old man becoming involved with their twenty-five-year-old sister. For her sake and his. No one was telling him what to do, but....

He'd backed off. When she'd questioned him about it, his carefully rehearsed speech hadn't gone well. Calling him a condescending jerk had been the mildest of the insults she'd hurled at him.

Now they barely spoke to each other. That was for the best, since no matter how many names she called him and how unwise a relationship would be, he still yearned for her.

Pulling into a parking area marked off with railroad ties, he grabbed his duffle from the passenger seat and put on the Stetson he'd taken to wearing whenever he was off duty.

The refreshing scent of the ginormous twin pines on either side of the flagstone walkway filled the truck's cab the minute he opened the door. Sunlight sparkled on the droplets clinging to the dark green needles. Must have rained here overnight. Hadn't noticed it at the station.

He took his time going up the walk, savoring the pleasure of coming back to his little piece of heaven. He wouldn't choose to live anywhere else.

As a city kid growing up in New Jersey, he'd played with an old set of Lincoln Logs and dreamed of having a cabin like this. He'd jumped at the chance to move in last spring. His favorite season had come around again and he planned to enjoy the hell out of it.

A week ago he'd hung up the porch swing and set out the table and chairs. Maybe he'd brew some coffee, grab a couple of sugar cookies from the batch Kendall had given him, relax on the swing, and watch the light change on the snow-capped Sapphires.

The fragrance of cedar firewood greeted him when he opened the door. Sunshine poured through the windows, bathing the floor-to-ceiling, multi-colored rock wall framing the fireplace. *Home.*

Closing the front door, he took his duffle to his bedroom and headed for the kitchen to start the coffee. He grabbed the glass carafe, crossed to the sink and stepped on the mat in front of it. The mat squished.

He glanced down. Water oozed up around the sole of his boot. Shoving the carafe onto the counter, he eased away from the mat and crouched in front of the wood cabinets that lined the wall.

His gut tightened. A water stain darkened the base of the cabinets on either side of the sink. The honey-colored wood had turned the shade of walnut. When he picked up the dripping mat, he was sick to his stomach. The wide-plank hardwood floor underneath had swollen and buckled.

Which meant the water had been sitting there a while. Anxiety tightened his throat. Could the damage be fixed? Maybe, but matching the wood of the floorboards and the cabinets would be damned near impossible.

Replacing the mat, he rose to his feet and took a five-gallon bucket from the broom closet. The mat, rolled into a soggy cylinder, barely fit, but it was all he had.

He set it aside and hurried down the hall to snag all the towels from his bathroom. Had rain leaked in? Doubtful. Could be a pipe under the sink.

The kitchen wasn't flooded, so it had to be a small leak that had been dripping for at least a couple of days. Or more? Had he checked under the sink before he left for work three days ago?

No. Then again, it wasn't like anyone would expect that kind of hypervigilance. He needed to give himself a break. This wasn't his fault.

Easy to say, but as he mopped up the worst of the puddle, his jaw clenched and a headache dug into the back of his skull. Cheyenne might not expect to live in this cabin again, but he'd lovingly supervised the construction. He'd put in sweat equity in addition to all his savings.

When the towels had absorbed most of the water, Dallas opened the cupboard doors under the sink and peered inside. Completely dry.

The leak continued, though. Fingers of water slid out from the narrow space between the refrigerator and the cabinets. He held his breath and listened.

Drip, drip, drip.

Pushing a towel into the opening to stop the flow, he stood and used the flashlight on his phone. There it was. The water line to the fridge had ruptured.

He'd been so tickled with this fancy refrigerator Cheyenne had. Now it had turned on him.

After he'd shut down the water supply to the fridge, he called Cheyenne. His buddy had left the station this morning in high spirits, headed for Miller's Hardware. He and Kendall had planned to use his time off to paint the baby's room.

Dallas was about to ruin his day.

2

Starting her own business had been Angie McLintock's most brilliant idea to date. Hiring Kendall as her assistant had been her second most brilliant move. Wagon Train Handywomen operated on a flexible schedule, so when Kendall needed a day off to help Cheyenne paint the baby's room, Angie took a short vacation, too.

Since the rain had passed and the sun was out, she hopped in her truck for the short drive to her mom's. Buttermilk could use some exercise. She'd offered to help Kendall and Cheyenne paint, but three painters would be a crowd in such a small space.

At least, that was the reason Kendall had given, although clearly she was looking forward to spending time alone with Cheyenne. Angie understood that. She envied Kendall a little, to be honest.

If only her February gameplan had worked out, she and Buttermilk would be taking a ride with Dallas and Smoky on this beautiful morning. Uh-oh. He had the day off, too, didn't he? Kendall and Cheyenne's painting project must have sidetracked her from noting that detail.

What if he'd decided to take a ride, too? They hadn't run into each other at the barn yet because she'd learned his schedule and took her rides when he was on duty. Evidently her brain had stopped working today.

She could scrub her plan, except she'd called her mom to let her know she was coming over. She'd even mentioned she was eager to take Buttermilk out. If she abruptly cancelled, her mother might think something was wrong.

She took her foot off the gas. The location of her cabin gave her no reason to pass Dallas's place on the way over to her mom's. But in the past three months she'd perfected the art of driving in his direction just far enough to get a glimpse of his truck and then quickly doubling back.

Should she flip a U-turn and go check to see if he was there or not? He probably was. He'd want to sit and relax on his first day off. *On the porch swing, idiot.* From that vantage point he'd hear her truck. She'd have to drive on by, which would screw up going to her mom's.

Okay, he had to pass her place to get to the barn and she hadn't heard anyone drive by. She could have been in the shower, though. It would be just her luck to find that dark blue truck sitting there when she arrived. What a pain in the butt.

To think she'd been over the moon when he'd rented Cheyenne's cabin. Now she wanted him gone — from the ranch, the town, the state, the country. And the planet? Sure.

Because he still made her heart race, the rat. He'd stunned her speechless the night he'd stepped onto the bandstand during the fire department's bachelor auction fundraiser. Her one and only ogle was seared into her retina.

Nothing had interrupted her view of his broad chest except the suspenders holding up his turnouts. A year later, she could still close her eyes and play that video—arresting brown gaze, tempting half-smile, impressive pecs, a smattering of dark chest hair, beautifully defined abs... and the hint of a generous package under his turnouts.

That night she'd successfully hidden her reaction from her tablemates — her mom and Kendall. If either of them had noticed, they would have commented. They hadn't. She'd vowed to tell no one.

Then Fate, or rather Cheyenne and Kendall's romance, had landed Dallas practically at her backdoor. And he'd been interested in her, damn it. She knew that look. But she'd played it safe and pretended indifference.

Guaranteed her overprotective brothers would have kicked up a fuss when she was only twenty-four. Dallas had turned thirty-two in October. Biding her time until her birthday had allowed her to covertly observe his behavior. Since she'd given him no encouragement, he'd stopped trying to impress her.

Being ignored by a guy who'd previously shown interest was a novelty that increased his appeal. His strength of character was sexy. He was funny, too.

She'd eagerly awaited her twenty-fifth birthday. Her brothers couldn't object at that point. Kendall had been twenty-five when she and Cheyenne had fallen in love. Cheyenne had been going on thirty-one. Their age gap was almost identical to the one between her and Dallas.

Turned out her brothers weren't the problem. Dallas was. Evidently the birthday party had reminded him of how *young* she was. He was looking for someone *closer to his age.* Blech. What a loser.

She let out a breath. Sitting here in the middle of the road wasn't smart. Even if he wasn't at the barn, he could come along any time. So could one of her other family members. Might as well drive to the barn and find out whether—

Her phone chimed. Kendall's ring. She picked up the phone, let up on the brake and pressed gently on the accelerator. "Hey, there. Need help with that painting gig, after all?"

"The painting's on hold."

"On hold?" She put on the brakes. "But—"

"Cheyenne and I are at his cabin. Dallas came home to find a big puddle in front of the kitchen sink that's been there for days. The floor's—"

"Oh, *no.*" Her stomach cramped. "What—"

"Water line to the fridge."

"Damn it! How long did it—"

"Don't know. Got the base of the cabinets, too."

"Those gorgeous cabinets! And the *floor.* Cheyenne must be—"

"Are you in the middle of something? I didn't even think to—"

"I'm in the middle of the road. I was going over to Mom's to take Buttermilk out. Did you call Sylvia?"

"She's been and gone. Took plenty of pictures. Insurance will cover most of it, but Cheyenne's worried it'll never be the same. You're the only one he—"

"I'll be right over." It was the thing to do even if she dreaded interacting with Dallas. "Ask him to call Mom so she knows why I won't be arriving."

"I will. Thanks, Angie."

"See you in a few." She disconnected, swerved to the side of the road and made a U-turn. Her heart ached for Cheyenne. He loved that cabin even if he no longer lived there.

She'd like to pin the blame on Dallas but the ruptured line was just a stroke of bad luck.

There would be a deductible, but since Cheyenne would want her and Kendall to do the work, they'd drop their labor costs by the amount of the... uh-oh.

In the heat of the moment, she'd missed the implications of taking on this job. Helping out her darling brother came with a big ol' asterisk — steady contact with effing Dallas Armstrong.

Good thing Kendall was her sidekick. That would keep her on the straight and narrow. Kendall was still clueless. Which was unusual for her, but then she was preggers.

Normally she would have noticed her best friend's sudden interest in Dallas during the birthday celebration. She would have questioned the push to acquire a horse ASAP.

But her excitement over the baby had taken center stage in her life that week and was still the main item on the agenda, as it should be. When the Dallas plan had failed so spectacularly, Angie had chosen to keep quiet about it. Kendall didn't need negative energy when she was carrying a member of the next generation of McLintocks.

Consequently, there'd be no rubber cockroach in Dallas's cookie jar. His toothbrush wouldn't accidentally end up in the toilet bowl. And nobody would sprinkle chili powder in his underwear. Damn it.

3

Kendall had to go out to the truck and fetch her phone to call Angie, which gave Dallas a moment alone with Cheyenne. "I assume you'll hire her to do the repairs." He did his best to sound casual although his nerves twanged like loose guitar strings.

"Unless she can't for some reason. I trust her to do it right. She'll treat my place like it was her own."

"But she'll have to be here a lot, and—"

"No worries. Kendall will be working with her."

"Oh." If he'd imagined lending a hand and possibly mending their fractured relationship so they were talking again, that wouldn't be happening. "Forgot about that."

"I didn't. That's why I knew it would be okay."

"Guess so." Was that the front door opening? He dipped his head and stepped closer to Cheyenne. "Real quick — does Kendall know about—"

"She doesn't, thank God." Cheyenne lowered his voice. "Angie hasn't told her or she'd have landed into me by now."

"She'd be upset?" Must not have been the door since he hadn't heard it close.

"To put it mildly."

Not good news. That meant Cheyenne hadn't been speaking for his wife. Just the opposite. She wouldn't appreciate his actions. Uneasiness settled in the pit of his stomach.

"Anyway, I appreciate how you handled the situation so quickly. All of us do."

"I don't want to cause problems."

"Everyone knows that."

Except Kendall. Angie's best friend.

"I have to say, buddy, whatever you told her must have been the right thing. Worked like a charm."

"It was a touchy conversation."

The front door closed with a decisive click. "Angie's on her way," Kendall called out.

Why hadn't he heard it open? What if she'd come in a minute ago? Had she been eavesdropping? He'd know soon enough if she ripped into Cheyenne.

Just in case it might help, he'd cover their tracks. "I just explained to the lady that it's risky to use indoor extension cords for outdoor illumination. When I offered to pick up a more suitable cord from Miller's she was all sweetness and light." He turned toward the kitchen doorway as Kendall came through it. "Did you get ahold of her?"

"Sure did! She'll be here any minute. She was already in her truck and headed to the barn." She transferred her attention to Cheyenne. "You're supposed to call your mom and explain that she's coming here and might not take the ride, after all."

"Will do." Cheyenne pulled out his phone and moved away while he talked to his mother.

Dallas relaxed. Kendall was acting totally normal.

She turned back to him. "I'm guessing that was Mrs. Jenson using the wrong extension cord. She's notorious for doing that."

"Well, I'm onto her, now."

"Good to know. By the way, how's Smoky doing?"

"He's good. Real good."

"Then he's stopped nipping you?"

"He has, thanks to a couple of training sessions with Beau. Seems I need to be the alpha in the relationship."

"I had to learn that with Mischief, too. He used to be a handful, until Beau— hey, sounds like Angie's truck pulling in. She made good time."

"Sure did." Dallas tensed. How would Angie play this? She'd managed to avoid being anywhere near him for three months but now....

Cheyenne put away his phone. "Mom's coming over. She wants to see."

"I'm not surprised." Kendall glanced at her husband. "Since you wanted Angie to come over, you must be planning to hire us."

"I am. Only thing is, this job can't wait."

"Don't worry about the baby's room. This is more important."

"We'll get to it, sunshine. We'll—"

"What's this I hear about a leak?" Angie sailed into the kitchen and skidded to a stop. "Oh, crap, Cheyenne. Your floor...."

"We'll have to replace those boards, for sure."

"Yeah, but locating flooring that will blend in with what's been here for eight years — that's the tough part."

"I have faith in you, sis."

"Me, too." Dallas threw that in. It was true and he didn't want to stand there like a bump on a log.

Her sideways glance wasn't hostile, but he wouldn't call it friendly, either. "Thanks, but I'm not a miracle worker. And I know Cheyenne's standards. We might have to tear up quite a few undamaged planks if we want it to look good." She pointed to the worst spot. "That's where the mat was, right?"

"Yes, ma'am. It was there when I moved in, so I just left it." Despite the circumstances, he was happy to see her. She'd pulled her curly black mane into a ponytail. Running his fingers through her luxurious hair had been something he'd... nope, better get off that track.

"The mat was probably a good thing, in a way. Although it ruined this section, it kept the water from going everywhere and creating more damage."

"I guess it did." She clearly wasn't blaming him for this disaster. That was in character. She'd impressed him as fair-minded. And funny. And sexy....

She hunkered down and gazed at the base of the cabinets lining the wall. "This is a bigger problem than the floor. If the base of these cabinets is warped, and I'll bet it is, they'll have to come out."

Cheyenne groaned. "I love those."

She rose to her feet. "Am I remembering right that they were a bargain because they were discontinued?"

"Afraid so. That means mismatched cabinets or replacing all of them." He swung to face Dallas. "How do you feel about it?"

"Me? I'm just renting. I don't have a vote."

"You're not *just renting* and we both know it. I've been wondering when you'd ask me about a rent-to-own agreement."

Cheyenne had figured that out? It was news to him. Good news, though. "I was waiting until I had a decent chunk to offer as a down payment. I was getting close, and then—" *Don't mention the horse, doofus! Do you want Angie to think you blame her for your lack of funds?* "Then I decided there was no big hurry."

"But you want this to be yours eventually?"

"Yes." He checked on Angie from the corner of his eye to gauge her reaction to having him take up permanent residence here. Her expression was impossible to read, just as it had been for the past three months.

On the other hand, Cheyenne was an open book. He smiled, clearly pleased. "In that case, you have a vote. Do you want the cabinets to match?"

"In a perfect world, sure, but replacing all of them seems like a waste of some very nice cabinets."

Angie shoved her hands in the pockets of her jeans. "Clint just finished Mom's lamp and he hasn't started anything new yet. What if you get him to build replacements based on the old design?"

"I thought of that, and he'd be great if he's willing." Cheyenne sighed. "But he's slower than molasses. Even he says that. I can't ask Dallas to wait weeks or maybe even months before he has a working kitchen."

"Yes, you can." Patience was something he could offer. "You know how much I care about this place. Doesn't matter to me how long the repairs take. I'll wash dishes in the bathroom sink."

"That's very accommodating." Cheyenne turned to his sister. "Regardless of what happens with the cabinets, we need to start the demo now, which mucks up your time off."

"I'm okay with that." She glanced at Kendall. "You were going to paint, though."

"It can wait. We need to get on this now. Since I dressed for painting this morning, I'm set to go."

"Dallas and I will help," Cheyenne said. "Right, buddy?"

"Absolutely." He hated the damage to the kitchen, but loved the idea that Angie would be around for the next three days. Who knew? Maybe by the end of that time she'd stop treating him like something she'd stepped in out in the pasture.

4

Angie was fine with Cheyenne's help but too bad he and Dallas came as a set. "Great. You can take stuff to the dump." That would get him out of her hair for a while. Then she could send him to Miller's for something or other. And lunch. He could fetch that from town.

"Whatever you need," Dallas said.

Ha. She needed nothing from him. Not anymore. Except to stay out of her sight. She'd written him off as a lost cause.

Unfortunately, whenever she was forced to be in his company, she couldn't help but notice those warm brown eyes and that muscular, I'm-good-in-bed body. Her rebellious libido hijacked her brain and activated her hormones.

Even now, when she should be concentrating on the sad state of Cheyenne's kitchen, she was in danger of hyperventilating because Dallas was close enough to catch the scent of his aftershave. Time to escape. "I need to run home, change clothes and grab my tools."

"I'll go with you," Kendall said. "I can load the truck while you change."

"Good idea. We're outta here." She headed for the front door and met her mom coming in. Not the polished Desiree McLintock the world saw, either.

She was in working writer mode, her copper curls sticking out every which way and her gray sweats and sweatshirt frayed from countless washings. "How bad is it?"

"It's not good. Kendall and I are heading to my place to fetch tools."

"So much for the painting project." Her mom gave Kendall a sympathetic smile.

"I'm not upset. We have four whole months before she shows up."

"Don't remind me. I wish it was four days. Anyway, after talking to Cheyenne I alerted Marybeth. She's bringing lunch around noon."

"Thanks, Mom." Now she couldn't send Dallas on that errand, but turning down a Marybeth lunch just wasn't done. The food would be amazing, better than anything from town.

"She can't stay away any more than I can. I'm gonna go check on those boys. See ya." She hurried toward the kitchen.

"Those boys," Kendall muttered as she followed Angie through the door and closed it behind her.

"I know." She clattered down the steps. "To her, they'll be boys forever."

"Wait 'til you hear what *those boys* have been up to."

She screeched to a halt. "Huh?"

"Let's get in the truck. When I tell you, you'll raise a ruckus, and I don't want them to hear you."

"What the hell?"

"Just get in the truck." Kendall quickened her step as they neared Angie's green F-150 sitting at the end of the flagstone walkway next to her mom's purple F-350.

She quickly climbed behind the wheel and fastened her seatbelt. "What's going on?"

"In a minute." Kendall fluttered her hand toward the ignition. "Get us out of here, first."

"You sure are acting weird." She turned the key and glanced at her best friend. "Buckle up, baby momma, or this truck's going nowhere."

"I will, I will." She clicked the belt in place before leaning against the headrest with a deep sigh. "Man, I just hate this."

"Is the belt that uncomfortable?" She backed around and pulled out. "Because if it is, I think they make an extension for—"

"It's not the belt. It's my husband. He—"

"Oh, no, you had a fight."

"Not yet, but I feel one coming on." She scooted around so she could look at her. "Did you make a play for Dallas on your birthday?"

Oh. "What do you mean?"

"Did you flirt with him? Looking back, I think you did."

"Kind of. No big deal."

"Seems like it to me. You've never flirted with someone who lives in town, let alone on this ranch. You have a rule against it."

"Rules are made to be broken, right?"

"But this was one you've had for years. You wouldn't have broken it without giving it a lot of thought. Was helping him choose Smoky part of the plan?"

"In a way, but it doesn't matter, anymore. Why are you asking about it so long after the fact?"

"Because I had preggers brain and completely missed that you'd zeroed in on him. I need to get the story."

"Is this the thing I'm supposed to raise a ruckus about? Because it's old news and I—"

"This is the thing I want to nail down before I tell you the thing you'll start yelling about. Do you or do you not have the hots for Dallas?"

She blew out a breath. "Yeah, okay, I did, past tense." And present tense, but she wasn't admitting that to anyone, not even her best friend.

"Angie! Why didn't you tell me?"

"Because you would've insisted I go for it. And I was only twenty-four, so it seemed smarter to wait until—"

"Your birthday. That's just like you. But I wish you'd said some—"

"I wasn't sure I would go through with it, and now I wish I hadn't. It was a mistake. He's not for me."

"Why?"

"Because he's a condescending jerk who flat-out told me I'm too young for him."

Kendall gasped. "Oh. My. God. When did he say that?"

"After we unloaded Smoky and settled him in his stall. I suggested taking a ride sometime soon. He glanced away, cleared his throat and gave me a speech about how I'm a nice person and he's grateful for my help with Smoky but he's not interested in a romantic relationship. He's looking for someone closer to his age."

Kendall made a sound low in her throat, like the warning of an attack dog poised to lunge. "My husband is in *so* much trouble."

"What's he got to do with it?"

Silence.

"Kendall?"

"Pull over."

"Are you carsick?"

"No. I think we need to be stationary for this part of the conversation."

"Okay." She moved to the side of the road, cut the engine and swiveled to face her friend, whose eyes were shooting sparks. "Why is Cheyenne in trouble?"

"Because he's the reason Dallas gave you that speech."

"What?"

"He convinced Dallas to back off and clearly used the age thing."

"Are you kidding me?"

"I can't *believe* he did that, not after—"

"Are you sure? How did you find this out?"

"I overheard them. Right after I called you, I came in the house and they were murmuring, like it was something I wasn't supposed to hear. First I heard my name, Dallas asking if I knew. Then Cheyenne said *Angie hasn't told her. She would have landed into me by now.*"

The breath left her lungs.

"I held the door open and just stood there, listening. Cheyenne told Dallas he appreciated the way he'd handled the situation so quickly and then he said *we all do*."

The shock hit first, stunning her into rigid silence. There were no words. Then anger surged, flooding her with heat and adrenaline.

"Damn him! I'm frickin' twenty-five years old, the same age as you were when—"

"I'm spittin' nails. Ready to whale on *all* of them. Who the hell do they think they are thinking they can—"

"But what about Dallas? He just rolled over! Talk about a spineless, gutless—"

"Yeah, yeah, he should have put up a fight, but—"

"No buts about it! He let Cheyenne talk him out of dating me. That stinks."

"I agree with you, it does." Some of the fire left Kendall's gaze. "Then again, if you look at it from his viewpoint...."

Angie sucked in air. "You're saying that because he has to work with Cheyenne and he's the new guy."

"And those firefighters are a loyal bunch."

"I know, but—"

"On top of that, he's renting Cheyenne's precious cabin. We just found out today he loves it so much he wants to buy it. He—"

"So he throws me over for a *house*?"

"Well, you have to admit it's a very nice house."

"*Ken*dall!"

"Just trying to lighten up this awful conversation. You know it's more than the house. He comes from a big family and I'm sure he misses them. It's the whole enchilada."

"Rowdy Ranch." She heaved a sigh.

"Bingo. Your mom treats him like one of her kids. Your brothers include him in stuff. The only McLintock who wasn't super friendly was you. Until your birthday."

"Because I knew my brothers would carry on if I made my move any earlier."

"You're probably right. But you can see how Dallas might be reluctant to get crossways with his best friend in Wagon Train so he can hang out with a woman who barely noticed he was alive until her birthday."

"My *twenty-fifth* birthday! My brothers are such hypocrites. It's fine for Cheyenne to get involved with you when you're only twenty-five, but—"

"I'm not their little sister."

"That shouldn't—"

"I know, I know. It shouldn't make a difference, but it does and none of them are thinking logically and I still have a score to settle with Cheyenne. He had no business—"

"He's not the only one involved. Not if he said *we all do*. Every single one of those *boys* shares responsibility for this."

"Thanks for the reminder. The body count just went up."

"You know what? Let me handle it. Your little munchkin doesn't need this nonsense upsetting her cozy world. She's probably got herself wound up as it is, without—"

"No, ma'am, you're not tackling this alone. My husband led the charge and didn't dare tell me about it. He knew I'd have a pan-fried hissy fit."

"And now we're supposed to rush to the rescue because his fancy refrigerator leaked all over his kitchen?"

"There's that."

"I'm ready to tell him where he can put that busted water line. And his warped cabinets and buckled flooring, too."

"Sounds fair to me."

"But I can't do it. Leaving the job to someone who might botch it would hurt my soul. His place is gorgeous and I know how to fix it so it'll stay that way."

"Can't argue with that."

"I won't be doing it for my brother. I'll be doing it for the cabin's sake." She glanced at Kendall. "Are you with me?"

"Of course. But first we gotta open up a can of whoop-ass on your brothers. Maybe even call a family meeting so we can publicly humiliate all of them. Come to think of it, your mom should've noticed you batting your eyelashes at Dallas."

"She might have except she'd just found out that two more granddaughters are on the way."

"So true. Timing is everything."

Angie gazed at her. "And maybe in this case it'll work in our favor. Thanks to this leak, you uncovered their dastardly deeds. But they don't know that."

"They certainly don't." Kendall's eyes glittered. "Are you suggesting we keep that info to ourselves for a while?"

"I am."

"Which gives us time to plot our revenge?"

"Exactly."

5

Dallas had volunteered his truck for the trip to the dump and it was piled high by late afternoon. The demo had lasted all day except for the lunch break, a delicious feast he would have enjoyed more if Angie hadn't mostly ignored him while she chattered away with her brother and Kendall.

Cheyenne rode shotgun on the drive to the town's landfill. "I hated tearing out those cabinets, but at least we salvaged the countertop and the drawers."

"That's something, anyway. Have you asked Clint about making replacements?"

"Not yet. I'd rather not bother him at work. But speaking of the Fluffy Buffalo, I'm taking Kendall and Angie out for dinner tonight. They both deserve it. You're welcome to come along."

"I dunno, buddy. That might be asking for trouble."

"I don't know why. Angie's certainly not interested in you anymore."

"That's for damn sure. I didn't expect her to make conversation while we were working, but she didn't say more than two words to me at lunch.

No, I take that back. She said four. *Please pass the coleslaw.*"

Cheyenne grinned. "You were hogging that coleslaw."

"Because it's the best I've ever had, which is saying something. My dad makes a great coleslaw."

"Have you invited your family to come out and visit?"

"I have, but to hear them talk, Montana might as well be on the moon. Or in an episode of *Wild Kingdom.* They're convinced grizzlies and wolves lurk in the shadows waiting to snack on tourists from New Jersey."

"Can't blame those critters. New Jersey tourists are so doggone tasty."

"See, that's why I haven't pushed it. Sure as the world someone would make a comment like that and my folks would be on the first plane headed east."

"Do they drive on the New Jersey Turnpike?"

"All the time."

"Then tell them they're ten times safer on Rowdy Ranch than on that fourteen-lane monster."

"You've been on it?"

"No sir, but I've seen pictures on the news and there's no way you'd catch me on that road. You gotta be nuts to drive on that."

"I guess it's all in what you're used to." He chuckled. "But I'll tell 'em what you said. I'd love to get my mom and dad out here. And my little brother, Ben. I know he'd like it once he sees how beautiful it is."

"Do you call him little because he's short or because he's young?"

"Oh, he's not short. Just young. Twenty-six." A year older than Angie. He did get the point Cheyenne had made three months ago. If Ben suddenly took up with a thirty-three-year-old woman, he'd worry a little.

That said, Angie didn't act her age. She owned a business and managed it well. He'd been tempted to say that.

But Cheyenne's other comment, that her relationships tended to be brief, had hit close to home. Her interest in him had come out of the blue and had already faded just as quickly. That wouldn't work for him.

"So what do you think? Want to join us at the Buffalo? Have some food, drink some beer? I mean, except Kendall."

He was torn. He hadn't spent an evening at the Buffalo since the night of Angie's party. Hadn't wanted to stir up the memory of how cute she'd been orchestrating her birthday line dance. Then she'd delivered a speech that had broken through the roadblock keeping Clint and Tyra apart.

"House Wine is filling in for The Beat-Up Trucks again. I like that the two bands are trading off, now."

"They are?"

"You didn't know that? What have you been doing with yourself?"

"Working. Puttering around here. Riding Smoky." Trying to forget about Angie. Maybe if he went tonight he'd finally get it through his head that she wasn't right for him. He'd never spent so much time agonizing over a woman he hadn't even kissed, let alone taken to bed. "Okay, sure. But we're splitting the bill."

"If you insist."

"And I'll drive myself and meet you there."

"You probably should. I'll be stuffing Angie in the tiny back seat of my truck and I doubt either of you would appreciate being mashed together in that cramped space."

She'd likely hate it, but he wouldn't mind at all.

* * *

Dallas arrived a few minutes late on purpose. Late was better than early. He could end up sitting at the four-top alone like some eager beaver. Instead he walked in and sauntered casually over to the table. Cool. Collected. Like a guy who'd driven the New Jersey Turnpike more times than he could count.

Cheyenne gave him a big smile. "There he is! I ordered you a beer. We didn't want to order food until you got here."

"Thanks." He pulled out the empty chair across the table from Cheyenne, which put him between Angie to his left and Kendall to his right. He had a view of the dance floor while Cheyenne had his back to it. "Thanks for the primo seat."

"No problem, buddy. Glad you could make it." He looked relaxed and happy.

Angie? Not so much. Maybe he shouldn't have come. But there was no backing out, now.

"I wouldn't mind waiting on the food. I'm still full from lunch." Shrugging out of his jacket, he hung it over his chair, but he kept his Stetson on. So had Cheyenne. The local habit of wearing a hat indoors, specifically for a night out at the Buffalo, had taken some getting used to.

"Marybeth puts out a great spread." Kendall picked up her menu. "But now that I'm eating for two, I'm always hungry. I'm going for the burger and fries."

"Same here." Angie closed her menu and pushed it aside. "I don't know why I even bother looking."

Dallas glanced at her, careful to keep his expression friendly but not too friendly. Tough to do when her hair hung past her shoulders in all its ebony glory and she'd dressed in a blue satin shirt that matched her eyes. "You wouldn't rather have a steak?"

"Nope." She met his gaze and for a split second there was...

A flare of attraction? His pulse leaped.

Then she looked away. "When I'm here, I'd rather dance than eat."

"Seems like you could do both." Had he imagined that fiery spark in her eyes? He wanted her to look at him again.

But she clearly wasn't going to. "Steak complicates things." She unfolded her napkin and laid it in her lap. Then she sipped some water, her dark lashes lowered, before focusing her attention on the bandstand where House Wine was setting up.

"Why does it complicate things?"

"It just does." She kept her head turned away.

"She picked up that tip from me." Kendall jumped in. Likely she'd taken pity on him. "Think about it. Steak demands more cutting, more chewing, and God forbid you let an expensive steak get cold while you're tearing up the dance floor."

"I see."

"And guaranteed Angie will be out there since House Wine is playing tonight." Cheyenne hooked a thumb over his shoulder. "Ever since her birthday she's been partial to them, right sis?"

"Right." She turned to her brother. "If you hadn't suggested this, I was going to."

"Then I'm glad I did. I'm grateful for all the work you and Kendall put in today. Awesome job."

"You're welcome."

"Gratitude and platitudes are all well and good," Kendall said, "but wait'll you get the bill. It'll be a doozy."

"Charge whatever you want. Insurance will cover the bulk of it. Knowing you, you'll keep the tab under what the insurance company pays out."

"I'm not talking about money." Kendall winked at Angie and Angie ducked her head.

But she didn't move fast enough. He caught her mischievous smile. He wasn't sure what the exchange between those two was all about, but they likely had inside jokes just like the firefighters at the station. Good to know she hadn't checked her sense of humor at the door when she'd come here tonight.

What he wouldn't give for one of her smiles directed at him. She'd been generous with them during the precious few days of horse shopping. He'd abandoned the idea of dating her, but couldn't they at least be friends? First he'd have to get her to like him again, though. Maybe—

"So, Dallas, which band do you like best, the Trucks or House Wine?" Kendall's voice derailed that train of thought.

"I can't say. I've only heard House Wine play that one song the night of the party."

"Seriously?" Her eyebrows rose. "I don't know how you've missed them. They're here as often as the Trucks. I can't choose a favorite. I like them both."

"I'm sure I will, too." He'd been at the table less than ten minutes and he'd already learned something valuable. Angie would rather dance than eat.

Rance brought their drinks over and Cecily took their orders for burgers and fries. Dallas grabbed the chance to covertly assess the Friday night dinner crowd that surrounded them. All couples.

Made sense that single folks with limited income would show up later, ordering only drinks and munchies while scoping out potential dance partners. For the next hour or two, he might be Angie's only choice. Would her love of dancing overcome her aversion to him?

6

A half-baked revenge plot might be worse than no plot at all. Bottom line, Angie was ill-prepared for the first round, an evening at the Buffalo with yummy Dallas Armstrong.

In the short time before she and Kendall had driven back to the scene of the disaster, they'd come up with one solid goal — to make the McLintock boys suffer. But they hadn't settled on how to accomplish that task.

Although they'd agreed that Dallas wasn't a target since he'd been put in a no-win situation, he was in danger of getting caught in the crossfire. If he did, well that was unfortunate, but then again, he'd picked the wrong side.

Once they'd returned to the cabin, the demo had absorbed all her attention. A private discussion with Kendall was out of the question with Cheyenne and Dallas on site. But the guys' thirty-minute trip to the dump had provided time to nail down an initial strategy.

Since Dallas clearly wanted to mend fences, Angie would gradually appear to thaw. The slow-drip process should begin to make her brothers nervous.

But the devil was in the details. The plan called for a slow thaw. One look at that cowboy in his yoked Western shirt and snug jeans had turned her into a puddle of lust. She was very much afraid he'd noticed her melting.

Time to shove her libido into cold storage, and fast. But how? Just as she'd begun to despair that her thermostat would be stuck on high forever, Clint showed up.

He gave Cheyenne a sympathetic smile. "Understand you had some bad luck, bro." Then his gaze swept the table. "Bet you're thankful you have this crew working on it."

"I am. They've put in a long day."

"But the worst is over." Angie had caught the slight hesitation in Clint's gaze as he'd taken in her proximity to Dallas. Just the arctic blast she needed to refocus. "Dallas and Cheyenne were a huge help getting the cabinets out of there."

Clint blinked. "You took out all of them?"

"Not yet," Cheyenne said. "Just the water-damaged ones. We saved the drawers and countertop in case—"

"I'd build you some matching replacements. I heard. I'm willing, but as you know, I'm not the fastest woodworker on the planet. You wouldn't have a working kitchen for—"

"I don't care." Dallas nudged back his hat. "And I'm the one living there. I'd rather be inconvenienced than see all those beautiful cabinets ripped out."

"Then I guess we have a deal."

Cheyenne let out a sigh of relief. "Thanks, Clint. I didn't realize how much I loved those cabinets until you said that."

"Happy to do it. Just want to manage expectations."

"I see this as win-win," Angie said. "It takes the pressure off Kendall and me. There's no rush on the floor if we're waiting for the cabinets." Even better, a leisurely pace presented so many more opportunities to mess with her brothers.

"Oh, I agree. Perfect solution." Mischief danced in Kendall's gaze. "We can do an hour here, an hour there, maybe even work in the evenings if Dallas doesn't mind."

"Not at all. You're welcome anytime. I'll get you a key."

"That would be lovely." She resisted the urge to giggle. Neither of her brothers were enjoying this conversation.

"Evenings?" Cheyenne gave his wife a not-so-happy look.

"Absolutely. Angie and I are a team. You wouldn't want me to abandon her."

"I wouldn't mind going solo for this one, Ken." She twisted the knife. "I don't want to rob you of quality time with my brother."

"On the other hand, I could hang out with Dallas while you two do your thing." Cheyenne's quick glance at Clint said it all.

His twin had a lovely frown on his handsome face. "I do hate for Dallas to go weeks living in a construction zone."

"Honestly, it's fine. I—"

"You're a good sport, but I'm gonna step up my game so we can get this show on the road. I'll be over tomorrow to pick up the drawers and measure the space."

"Great." Angie gave him a big smile. "Kendall and I will be there making decisions about the floor. Cheyenne, I'm sure you'll want to be part of that discussion."

"Yes, ma'am."

"And obviously I'll be there," Dallas said.

"Then I'll see you all in the morning." Clint touched two fingers to the brim of his Stetson. "Enjoy your meal."

"We will, plus the dancing!" Kendall called after him. Then she turned to her husband. "Speaking of which, let's go. I love this song." She gave Angie a parting wink as she tugged a clearly reluctant Cheyenne out on the floor.

Crunch time. What next in the slow-thaw program they'd outlined? Maybe a lukewarm apology was in order. Turning to Dallas, she cleared her throat. "Look, the last time we talked in private, I said some things that—"

"So did I. How about we forget about that for now? Let's dance."

"Uh...okay." Her cheeks grew warm. "If you want to."

"Don't you? You said you'd rather dance than eat."

Yep, she'd painted herself into that corner. She'd been fighting her attraction instead of strategizing and that comment had popped out. Offering to be her dance partner was the gentlemanly thing to do now that they'd been left alone at the table. "I did say that, but you aren't obligated to—"

"No obligation, here. It'll be fun, just like last time."

"This isn't a line dance."

"Not that one. We danced together at the Rowdy Roost party."

"Oh. Right." She'd pushed that hot memory to the back of her mental closet.

"At the moment, I'm your best bet for a partner. The room's full of happy couples." He stood and offered his hand.

Dancing with him was risky, but it would stick a burr under Clint's saddle. She checked out the bar.

He stood behind it mixing drinks and pretending that he wasn't keeping an eye on her. But his quick sideways glance gave him away. She slid her hand in Dallas's. "Then I guess you're stuck with me."

"And vice-versa." He led her to the dance floor and drew her expertly into his arms. "But just to be clear — if there were a hundred single women in this room, I'd still rather dance with you."

Her heart did a stutter-step. If he'd agreed to back off, he shouldn't be saying things like that. "Because I'm good at it?"

"That's one reason." He tightened his grip on her waist and executed a fancy spin.

"Too bad I'm so young." Being a smartass was her only defense. Close contact with his virile body robbed her of breath and sent her pulse into overdrive.

"Too bad I'm so old." He twirled her around again.

She gulped for air. "At least you're spry for your age." He wasn't even breathing fast, the rat.

"I stay active." He flashed her a grin. "Having fun, yet?"

Oh, yeah. Way too much fun. "More than I expected, considering."

"That I'm a condescending jerk?"

"You were."

"I know." The music ended, but he didn't release her. "Angie, I'm sorry."

She made the gigantic mistake of looking into his deep brown eyes. Regret shone there. Regret and something more potent. She glanced away, but it was too late to control her response, a moist ache, a craving she'd been battling for months.

The band launched into another number and he still had his arm around her waist. "Want to— "

"Not right now." She couldn't risk dancing with him when she wanted to jump his bones. She gestured toward their table, conveniently loaded with four plates of food. Timely delivery. "Let's go eat."

"Okay." He sounded disappointed.

Join the club. She'd spent three months mired in disappointment. And months prior to that working hard to hide her attraction.

Her overwhelming reaction to him the night of the bachelor auction had caught her off-guard. When he'd walked on stage, her hormones had shouted *this one.* More than a year later, she still wanted him and only him, to the point that she'd stopped dating. His unexpected rejection had devastated her.

The rejection hadn't been his idea, but he'd cooperated with her brothers' bonehead plan. The past three months had been hell. It was payback time.

7

Right after Dallas and Angie took their seats, Kendall and Cheyenne came back to the table.

"Call the *Sentinel*," Kendall announced. "For the first time in history, I'd rather eat than dance." Much teasing followed and Kendall leaned into it by moaning with pleasure over each bite she took.

Although Dallas laughed and joked with everyone else while he ate his meal, his focus was elsewhere. Against all odds, Angie still wanted him. The look she'd given him on the dance floor had hit him like a wall of flames.

Clearly she wasn't comfortable with her reaction, maybe because she didn't like him all that much. Who could blame her after what he'd said three months ago? And now that they'd worked side-by-side on the demolition project, he questioned the assumptions that had convinced him to deliver that obnoxious speech.

When Cheyenne had broached the touchy subject in February, he'd put great emphasis on the age difference, a difference nobody could dispute. It was a fact. But did it matter? The woman he'd seen in action today had the maturity and dedication of someone years older.

She also had the skill and knowledge to manage a successful business, not something many twenty-five-year-olds could say. No wonder she and Kendall were in demand. Cheyenne was damned lucky to have a person of her caliber repairing his place.

As for her flaky dating habits, he was calling bullshit on that, too. If she collected and discarded men in the helter-skelter way Cheyenne had suggested, she would have latched onto another guy right after he'd bowed out.

As angry as she'd been that day, she would have made sure he was aware she'd moved on to someone else. He wasn't a relationship expert, but he knew that much. If she'd been involved with anyone in the past three months, he'd eat his Stetson.

But guaranteed she'd nursed a grudge against him during that time. And rightly so. Which put him in the middle of a very sticky situation.

If he told her why he'd made that speech, he'd betray his best friend at the station, the man whose cabin he rented, the guy who'd introduced him to the McLintocks. He'd grown to love that family. And yet, what right did Angie's brothers have to interfere with her romantic choices?

None whatsoever.

Kendall polished off the last of her burger and fries. "Let's order dessert."

Cheyenne's eyebrows rose. "You have room?"

"Not yet, but I will after we dance another fast one. We can order it now and it'll be sitting here when we get back. I'll have another glass of iced tea, too, please."

"You got it, sunshine." He glanced around the table. "Four slices of chocolate layer cake?"

Angie gave him a thumbs-up. "Works for me."

"Me, too, buddy. I never leave the Buffalo without having their chocolate cake."

Cheyenne placed the order and added another round of drinks. "That's done." He looked at Angie and Dallas. "You guys ready to get back out there?"

Would Angie dance with him again? No telling. As he hesitated, she shocked the heck out of him with a jaunty *sure* and a breezy smile.

"Alrighty, then." He tucked his napkin next to his plate and pushed back his chair.

This time she led the way to the floor. The tune was familiar, Kane Brown's *Lose It,* and she began swaying to the rhythm before they hit the hardwood. When they reached it, she twirled to face him, her lustrous black hair sweeping past her shoulders.

He grabbed her — no other way to describe it — and took control of the situation. Or so he thought. But she wasn't having it.

She turned into a livewire, adding elements to the dance that left him gasping. Shimmying closer, she brushed him with the tips of her breasts. Before he could pull her in tight, she danced out of reach.

Then she was back, sliding her fingers through his, giving him a hip bump and a taunting smile. He tightened his grip but she wiggled free. Releasing his hand, she teased him with another mouth-watering shimmy and spun back into his arms with a low, sexy laugh.

He ran up the white flag, let her rule the dance, rule him. She could have anything she wanted. He vibrated to the beat, gazed into her eyes and dreamed of taking her home tonight.

Why not? What the hell? She was destroying her brothers' neat little program with this routine. Cheyenne and Clint must be having a collective cow. And he didn't give a damn if they were. This woman deserved to live her life any way she wanted.

He was panting by the time the number ended, partly from exertion, but mostly from a full-blown case of lust. The only reason it didn't show in an embarrassing display was that he'd been moving too fast to allow his blood to gather in one spot.

She was breathing fast, too, which made her lovely breasts tremble. "Like what you see, cowboy?"

Caught. He lifted his gaze. "Yes, ma'am, I do."

Her seductive smile turned him inside out. "Wait'll you watch me eat chocolate cake." She sauntered back to the table.

Wiping a hand across his mouth to make sure he wasn't drooling, he followed her. As they all sat down and started in on their fat wedges of the most decadent dessert on the menu, Kendall and

Angie launched into an animated discussion of who was sexier, Kane Brown or Chris Young.

Cheyenne didn't offer an opinion. Instead he slowly forked up bites of cake while staring across the table as if trying to parse out what had just happened. Dallas lifted his shoulders in a quick shrug. He'd had absolutely nothing to do with Angie's provocative dance. Innocent bystander.

Meanwhile Angie, the instigator, made good on her promise to tantalize him with her food. Her conversation with Kendall continued as before, but her method of eating cake had gradually moved into X-rated territory.

He tried to keep his attention on his plate. Really he did. But without blinders to block his peripheral vision, he couldn't avoid the deliberately erotic show.

Spearing a bite of cake with her fork, she proceeded to lick off every bit of the frosting with languorous movements of her tongue. Eventually she popped the sponge part in her mouth, chewed and swallowed. A new bite covered in creamy dark chocolate received the same treatment.

He adjusted his napkin in his lap and avoided looking across the table at Cheyenne. If they stayed for another dance, and he hoped to hell they would, he'd use that time to ask if he could take her home. He had a lot more than a kiss at the door in mind.

Perhaps Clint and Cheyenne expected him to reject the open invitation she'd issued. If so, they'd be disappointed. Any man who could resist Angie in seduction mode was a perfect candidate for the priesthood. He was not that man.

When everyone except Angie had finished their dessert, Kendall pushed back her plate with a happy sigh. "So delicious. And now I'm sleepy."

Yes. Cheyenne would have to take his baby-momma home early. But there was no reason for Angie to leave. After all, she still had cake. And a ride home.

Cheyenne's pained expression revealed his internal struggle.

Dallas pitied the guy. Angie seemed to find it amusing.

Taking a deep breath, Cheyenne turned to his wife. "I'll bet another dance will wake you up."

"Sorry, sweetheart, but I need to go to bed."

So did Dallas, for a different reason.

"Um, okay. Then I guess—"

"But first I have to pee. It's a long ride back. If you'll excuse me, I'll only be a minute." She scooted back her chair.

So did Angie. "I'll go with you." She gestured toward her beer. "It's the second bottle that does it."

The minute they left the table, Cheyenne leaned forward and lowered his voice. "I don't know what she's up to, but—"

"Yes, you do." He moved closer, too. "She's decided she likes me even if I did make a jerk of myself and tell her she was too young for me. Which she's not, by the way, and I—"

"Don't take the bait, buddy. I agree she's coming on to you. It's unusual for her to act that way when I'm around. Or when any of us are."

"Meaning your brothers?"

"Right. It's like she's trying to prove a point. To you, because she's still mad about what you said, but also to me. And Clint, since he's here."

"And Rance? He's here, too."

"Well, not so much Rance. He and Lucky, being closer to her age, tend to be neutral on the issue."

"Maybe she is trying to prove a point. And maybe she feels the need to because—" He straightened. "They're coming back. Just let me say this. If she decides to stay, I'll be taking her home. And I make no promises about what will or won't happen. She's not flighty when it comes to guys. She knows what she—"

"I'm telling you, it would be a mistake. She's just using you to—"

"Cool it."

Cheyenne settled back in his chair and picked up his beer. He didn't look happy.

Dallas wasn't happy, either. Getting crossways with his friend was no picnic. A lot was at stake. And Angie's expression gave him no clues as she approached the table.

Then she provided a ginormous clue by picking up her jacket from the back of her chair. "I'm ready to leave, too." She glanced at him, all teasing gone from her expression. "You're welcome to have the rest of my cake. See you tomorrow around nine, if that's okay."

"You're welcome to show up anytime." He gulped back his disappointment. Maybe Cheyenne was right. She'd only been making a point.

8

Kendall's ringtone woke Angie at seven the next morning. Normally she was up by then, but she hadn't slept well. She wandered into the kitchen where she'd left her phone and answered. "Hey."

"What took you so long?"

"I was asleep."

"Are you serious? The sun's up!"

"Rough night."

"Aw, I'm sorry. I was hoping you'd sleep the sleep of the just. You got those boys good last night."

"So why do I feel guilty about Dallas? He looked crestfallen when I told him I was leaving."

"Only because he thought you'd be leaving with him. But let's not forget that he—"

"Hang on a minute. You're talking like Cheyenne's not there. Where is he?"

"Out feeding the chickens and the horses. He loves handling those chores when he's off duty. Normally we do it together, but I had this super idea so I pretended to be tired so I could call you. We need to make a decision before he gets back."

"What's the idea?"

"Simple. I overdid with the demo yesterday and dancing last night and I need to take time off to recuperate."

"Did you really overdo it?"

"Of course not. But Cheyenne's never had a pregnant wife so what does he know? If I tell him I need to be babied for a couple of days, he'll drop everything and take care of me. He's cute that way."

"Then I'm supposed to go over there by myself this morning?" Her heart was excited and her tummy was nervous.

"Brilliant, isn't it? Since you'll be alone with him, you can act repentant about flirting with him. Be nice and thaw a little more. Find out where he stands at this point."

"Yeah, I have no idea, other than he's hot for my body." And hers issued a quick reminder that the feeling was mutual.

"And bonus, Cheyenne will worry about you working over there without me. You are still mad at Dallas, right?"

"Sort of. He did give up on me without a fight. Then again, I mostly ignored him for the first nine months he lived here, so he didn't have much skin in the game. I can see why he might have gone along with Cheyenne's request. But he looked sad last night. I felt mean for teasing him and walking away."

"Well now you can make amends. You can get a sense of whether he's rethinking his loyalties. Maybe you'll even decide to tell him the truth."

"Really? This soon into the campaign?"

"You be the judge, but if he acts like he might want to switch sides, you could level with him. You could even get cozy with him, but you'll have to be discreet. As in *very* discreet."

"Now I'm getting the shivers."

"Of course you are. You want him as bad as he wants you. Your brothers, including my darling husband, are idiots."

"I would agree."

"But if you do get horizontal, it'll raise the stakes, so be sure and let me know."

"In the moment?"

She laughed. "Dear God, no. But at some point. Don't call, though. Text me. Something cryptic."

"How about *I just saved a horse*?" On the other end Kendall completely lost it.

She was still giggling when she recovered enough to talk. "Listen, I should hang up so he doesn't catch me laughing and yakking on the phone when I'm supposed to be down for the count. I'll let him know I called you."

"Good. I—wait, I just remembered Clint's coming over first thing to measure the space and pick up the drawers. We won't be all alone, after all."

"Eventually he'll leave, though, either because he's scheduled to work at the Buffalo or because he needs to start on those cabinets. He has no reason to stick around."

"True."

"But speaking of Clint, I'll bet Cheyenne called him the minute he got to the barn and filled him in on this new development."

"Yep. And then Clint will text Bret who will text Gil and so on until they all know I won't have you helping me for a couple of days. I could have a parade of my brothers coming by to check on the progress. I mean check on *me.*"

"Just watch your step."

"Always. I'll keep in touch. Cryptically."

Kendall chuckled. "You do that." She disconnected.

After that scintillating phone call, Angie was wide awake. And for the first time since becoming the proprietor of Wagon Train Handywomen, she wondered what the heck to wear to work. Not so much the outfit, since practicality ruled on that score, but now she faced the potential of quality time with Dallas.

When he stripped away her sturdy pants and serviceable long-sleeved shirt, something sensual and seductive should be covering her lady parts. Might not happen today. Or tomorrow. Or ever. So much depended on his attitude.

Her longing for his sweet lips and muscular body drove her crazy, but not so crazy that she'd go to bed with him just to scratch that itch. He had to prove himself worthy.

* * *

Clint's gunmetal gray truck sat beside Dallas's dark green one when Angie pulled in a couple minutes before nine. Not surprising. Dollars to donuts Clint had arrived early to reinforce Cheyenne's evaluation of her wild dance last night.

Her brothers had pegged it, and she'd done a hell of a job working Dallas into a frenzy. The flush of victory had faded fast, though, leaving her depleted instead of energized. She couldn't wait to apologize and see where that discussion took them.

She picked up a small metal toolbox from the passenger seat. She'd left the rest of her tools in Dallas's kitchen but this compact beauty was always either in her cabin or in her truck. Never knew when an emergency would crop up and she'd be caught without a decent screwdriver or an adjustable wrench.

Toolbox in hand, she climbed out, shivering in the cold breeze. The temperature had dropped significantly during the night and she'd had to scrape frost off her windshield before driving over. It covered the windshield on Dallas's truck, too. Smoke curled from the cabin's rock chimney, bringing with it the aroma of a cedar fire. She could smell coffee brewing.

If Clint would vamoose, Dallas might offer her a cup of coffee. If not, she might be so bold as to ask for one. Then they could sit in front of the fire and talk about last night. She didn't have to start work on the floor immediately. Filled with good intentions, she rapped lightly on the door.

Dallas opened it, his gaze stern. "Morning." He stepped back, giving her room to slip past him, but he didn't exactly invite her in.

Now *he* was the angry one. Great. "Good morning to you, too." She gave him a quick smile on her way through the doorway. "It's just me today. Kendall—"

"So I heard."

Clint stood over by the fireplace, coffee mug in hand, hat nudged back, friendly as you please. "Hey, sis."

"Hey, big brother." She set her toolbox on the floor.

"Chilly out, huh?"

"Sure is." Not as chilly as Dallas when he'd greeted her at the door.

"Glad you're here. We've been discussing the cabinets."

Sure they had. And she was Elmer Fudd. Did Tyra know that her husband had been interfering with his sister's love life? Not likely.

To think Clint and Tyra had been on a runaway train to splitsville until Angie, her mom and Kendall had come up with a strategy to coax them back together. Some thanks she was getting for that act of kindness. Guaranteed the women in the family had been left out of the loop on this matter. That might need to change.

She pasted on a congenial expression. "Anything I need to know about the cabinets?"

"I'd like your perspective. I plan to copy the exterior as closely as possible, but the shelving can be different. I can make 'em so they roll out, like you did with yours. Have you had any issues with that feature?"

"Nope. I'm glad I converted them. But won't that take longer and be more work?"

"A little, but it'd be easier to do it now than after they're in. Dallas is all for it. Since he plans to buy the place and he's already said he doesn't care how long it takes, makes sense to do it the way he wants."

"What about the extra expense?"

He shrugged. "It'll be added labor, but the materials won't change much. Since it was my idea, doesn't seem fair to jack up the price."

Oh, boy. She finally got the picture. Her brothers could offer Dallas a treasure trove of goodies — discounts on custom cabinets, farrier service at a reasonable rate and vet bills that wouldn't blow his budget. The cabin he desperately wanted to buy would be offered to him below market value because he was a buddy and fellow firefighter.

Who wouldn't be thrilled with all that, especially when the woman he'd been asked to ditch had played him for a fool last night? Maybe she and Dallas were doomed, after all.

9

The silent undercurrent in the conversation between Clint and Angie swirled like dust motes in a shaft of sunlight. Dallas kept his mouth shut. Only a fool would get tangled up in whatever was going on between brother and sister.

Angie's stiff body language told him she was on edge. Cheyenne and Clint had both insisted she was still upset about his behavior three months ago, and that was probably true. But she wasn't directing her anger at him. It was focused on her brother.

Last night she'd clearly relished Cheyenne's negative reaction to her sexy dance. Had she been angry with him, too? Maybe, or maybe she sometimes enjoyed pulling his chain. Sibling relationships were complicated, as he well knew.

This morning she could be out of sorts for a million reasons, including insufficient caffeine. Hell, he was out of sorts. She'd done a number on him last night. He deserved it, but that didn't mean he had to like it.

Carrying his coffee mug, Clint started toward the kitchen. "I'll load up those drawers and be on my way."

"I'll help." Dallas followed him.

"You've already measured?" Angie called after them.

"Did that earlier," Clint said over his shoulder.

"Aren't you the eager beaver."

"I try, sis. I try."

Dallas was almost through the kitchen door before his hospitality training kicked in. He turned back. Angie was hanging her denim jacket on the coat tree by the door. He hadn't even offered to take it for her.

He cleared his throat. "Would you like a cup of coffee? I should have—"

"Thanks. I can get it. Go ahead and help Clint with the drawers. I'd help, too, but you guys can handle them just fine. You don't need me."

She was dead wrong, there. He wished he didn't need her, but every time he laid eyes on her, his internal GPS announced he'd arrived at his destination. "Okay. I'll be right back." Why had he said *that*?

But as he and Clint deposited the drawers in the bed of his gray F-250, he figured out why he'd promised Angie he wouldn't be long. They needed a private discussion. The sooner, the better.

He stepped away from the truck, eager to head inside. "Thanks again for taking this on. Oh, and thanks for bringing me a couple of ice cube trays. I'll need those for a while."

He must have telegraphed his intention, because, Clint blocked his escape and put a hand on his shoulder. "I can tell you're still attracted to her. Don't blame you. But trust me, she's never been serious about any guy. It's highly unlikely you would be any different. So—"

"I appreciate you sharing that." He shivered. "Guess I should have put on a coat. Cold out here." He edged backward, out of reach. "Anyway, I'll stay on my toes. Last night was a wakeup call."

"I can imagine."

A wakeup call and a rollercoaster. Maybe she'd always planned to toss him aside. But Clint hadn't seen the warmth in her eyes after their first dance last night. She'd clearly revealed more than she'd meant to before beating a quick path back to the table. That could explain the second dance and the rejection that followed.

Clint tugged his hat down. "Even though she's best friends with Kendall, they're nothing alike. Kendall was ready to settle down. Angie, not so much."

"Probably true." He took another step back, and another.

Clint gave him a nod. "I'll let you know how it goes with the cabinets."

"Thanks." He continued to backpedal toward the porch. "Can't wait to see how they come out." With a wave, he turned and bounded up the steps.

She was kneeling on the kitchen floor, sitting on her heels with her hands in her lap while she studied the wide planks that remained. He glanced around for her coffee cup. Evidently she'd decided not to accept his offer.

Without looking up, she gestured toward the gap where they'd taken out the warped boards. "I think we'll have to rip out a couple of good ones if we want to disguise the repair job. I hate to sacrifice more wood, but—"

"Do what you gotta do." He left his hat on the counter and dropped to his knees in front of her. Ah, the peppermint scent.

She didn't care for perfume. During those precious days spent negotiating the deal for Smoky and settling the gelding into the McLintock barn, he'd asked if she wore any. Nope. Just used peppermint soap, shampoo and toothpaste. Reminded her of Christmas.

She pointed to the exposed edge of a plank. "This is tongue-and-groove flooring, so in order to replace—"

"Angie, how do you feel about me?"

Her breath hitched but she kept her attention on the floor. "No comment."

She'd used a yellow scrunchie to put her dark curly hair in a ponytail. The glossy strands were still slightly damp. She smelled like a candy cane. "Do you feel the same as you did three months ago?"

"Yes." Her breathing picked up speed.

"Then you still want me to eat shit and die?"

No answer, just more quick breaths.

He wasn't breathing all that steadily, himself. He gripped his thighs so he wouldn't reach for her. "I'm asking because when you said it, you sounded very serious."

"Oh, I was." Her fingers tightened, her posture mirroring his as she pressed her fingertips into the sturdy cotton of her work pants.

Was she resisting the urge to grab him or smack him? Keeping his tone neutral took all his resources. "Hm."

"I hate it when someone goes *hm*. Say something or keep quiet." Her voice quivered. "Don't just make a noise that means nothing."

"Sounds to me like you have some strong feelings going on."

"What if I do?" She lifted her head, blue eyes hot as the flame on a gas stove, her pink lips parted as she sucked in air. Jaw tight, she leaned forward, getting in his face. "You annoy the *crap* out of me."

"Is that so?" Keep calm, dude. This is working.

"You sound like an effing psychologist, and then you exacerbate the situation with your know-it-all *hm*! Is that the best you've got? Probably! As we've established, you're older than dirt!"

"Exacerbate. What a great word. It has heft." Hallelujah, she was furious, as angry as she'd been three months ago.

"Do you have a point, Armstrong? Because if you don't, let me show you where I'm planning to take out the planks. If you agree, then I can get on with it."

"I do have a point." He cupped the back of her head. Her eyes widened. "This."

She gasped when he kissed her. The velvet luxury of her lips and candy-cane taste of her mouth snapped his control and he thrust his tongue deep, taking full advantage of her surprise. No excuse for it.

Except the truth. He craved this kiss more than his next breath. He'd take the consequences. She could do serious damage with her pearly whites. Or she could...

Like it? Welcome his tongue as a valued guest? Clutch his head and press her fingers into his scalp while she whimpered and kissed him back? Alrighty, then!

_10_

Hot damn. Angie threw herself into the kiss for all she was worth. One of her brothers could charge through the door any minute, but right now nothing mattered but the mouth-to-mouth connection she had going on with Dallas.

This was a kiss that was going somewhere, judging from buttons coming undone, his and hers. Her runaway heart thrummed in her ears, keeping time with the rasp of harsh breathing and feverish moans.

Lust saturated her brain, sending an urgent message to prepare a liquid welcome for the next phase. Clearly his erotic, penetrating kiss was the dress rehearsal for a more substantial invasion.

Sliding both hands inside his open shirt, she spread her fingers over the warm cotton t-shirt stretched across his lovely muscles. With a groan, he yanked the tail of her shirt free.

While he reached for the catch on her bra, she undid the metal button at the waist of his jeans. She'd pulled his zipper halfway down when his hand closed over hers.

He ended the kiss slowly, keeping a tight grip on her hand as he lifted his head.

"You're *stopping*?" She stared at him in disbelief.

"Yes, ma'am." His dark eyes glittered as he sucked in air. "Before we... do this... we have to talk."

"To hell with talking!" She gulped. "We still want each other and I'm sick of—"

"Me, too." He took her by the shoulders and gently shifted her weight so she was sitting on her heels again. Then he zipped his jeans and fastened the button at his waist. "But there's a lot on the line. For both of us."

He was right, and the venue wasn't secure. Kendall had warned her to be discreet. "More for you than me." She buttoned her shirt and he followed suit.

"How do you figure?"

She wasn't ready to get into it yet. "Why did you kiss me?"

He gave her a crooked smile. "Couldn't help it. You smell like Christmas. Taste like it, too."

"You couldn't resist me?" Nice to know.

"That's about the size of it."

"But then you *did* resist me. What made you stop?"

"The sound of my zipper. We were seconds away from doing it on the floor. Without a condom."

"No, we weren't."

"Then why did you pull down my—"

"Use your imagination."

His eyes widened.

"Ah, the light dawns. Just so you know, my mother educated us all on the wisdom of condoms.

You get me hot, but not hot enough to forget what was drilled into me."

"I see."

"Want to reconsider your decision to stop?" She managed to keep from laughing. Judging from the hunger in his gaze, she'd painted a picture that appealed to him.

But he heaved a sigh of regret. "This isn't the place."

"Probably not, but I'm sure you have a more appropriate place somewhere in this cabin."

"I do." He cleared his throat. "But—"

"Never mind. You did the right thing, calling a halt." Reaching behind her back, she hooked her bra, which sparked another flash of heat in his eyes. "We could have visitors at any moment."

The heat faded. "We probably will and before anybody shows up, I have some things I want to say."

"Coffee by the fire?"

"Works for me." Pushing to his feet, he held out his hand and helped her up. "I'll wrangle the coffee if you'll go check the fire."

"Meet you in there." She tucked in her shirt as she left the kitchen. Sounded like someone might be switching sides.

She had to walk around the kitchen table and chairs that had been moved into the living room in order to reach the fireplace. The flames had died down so she added another log. As she replaced the grate, Dallas came in with two steaming mugs of coffee and set them on the glass-topped coffee table.

"Which mug is mine?"

"Doesn't matter. I pulled out two clean ones. Fresh start."

"Then I'll take this one." She claimed the end of the sofa closest to the kitchen and picked up the mug sitting in front of her. "This is the side I used to sit on when Cheyenne lived here."

"Did you spend a lot of time in this house?" Dallas sat next to her but left a space between them.

"I did, as a matter of fact. Hey, you can sit closer, you know."

"Not really. I'm determined we're gonna talk."

She gave him a sideways glance. "I like it when you're determined. Very sexy."

"No fair."

"Okay, talk."

He dragged in a breath. "Just to be clear, I'm aware that I've interrupted your work."

"Which is okay because without cabinets there's no urgency to get the floor repaired. I'd like to get the materials ordered soon for my own peace of mind, but we have plenty of time. Now, if we already had the cabinets—"

"You wouldn't have kissed me back?"

"I wouldn't have participated in the discussion prior to you kissing me. I wouldn't have let myself get sidetracked by your highly personal questions."

"Because you're a professional." It was a statement, not a question.

A gratifying statement. She shifted her position so she could look at him. Never a hardship, but far more pleasurable when he said things like that.

"Seems you were right. I've been a condescending jerk."

"It's lovely to hear you say that, but I don't get what's changed. We're each three months older, so technically I'm still too young for you."

"Which is nonsense. In less than two years you've created a thriving business from scratch. That's impressive."

'Then starting a business has aged me?"

He flushed. "I didn't mean—"

"I'm teasing. But to be fair, I didn't really start from scratch. I hired on at Miller's Hardware when I was eighteen. Most of my clients are former customers I helped with home repair issues over the four-plus years I worked there. Going out on my own was a no-brainer."

"And gutsy."

"I suppose that much is true."

"The thing is, I haven't paid attention. That's on me. I didn't see that about you until yesterday, when the dedicated professional showed up at my door. You called it. Condescending jerk."

She smiled. "You were blinded by my beauty. I get that a lot."

"I was, but that's no excuse."

"I was kidding."

"I'm not. I noticed you the minute I moved in here, but you didn't seem to—"

"Yes, I did, but I didn't want anyone to know, including you. You've had my full attention ever since the bachelor auction."

His jaw dropped. "You were there?"

"Of course. Cheyenne was in it. Or rather, he was supposed to be and then Clint—"

"Took his place. Like we wouldn't guess. I dreaded that auction almost as much as Cheyenne, but now I'm grateful. Without it he wouldn't be married to Kendall and I wouldn't be living in this cabin." He studied her. "So why did you avoid me when I moved to the ranch?"

"It's a long story."

"I'm listening."

"Ever since I started dating, I've chosen guys from out of town so they wouldn't have to run the gauntlet of my brothers."

His gaze sharpened.

"I kept the relationships casual. I didn't want a serious relationship while I was figuring out who I was, what I wanted my life to look like. And guaranteed my brothers wouldn't be happy if I'd tied myself down at an early age, so there was that."

"Hm." Then he grinned. "Sorry. I'll work on that."

"I don't really hate it. In fact, I kinda like hearing that sound. Makes me want to kiss you."

"Hmmm."

"Okay, then." She put down her mug. "I guess the story can wait."

"No, it can't." He set his mug next to hers and wrapped his arm around her. "But let's get cozy so I can kiss you when it's over."

She snuggled against him. "I'll make it quick. I started my business, I attended the auction, you moved here and...."

"Nothing. Why nothing?"

"Because you were seven years older and I was only twenty-four. I was afraid my brothers would raise a ruckus and things would get messy. Then I turned twenty-five. How could they object? Kendall was twenty-five when she and Cheyenne got together. So I made a play for you."

He pulled her in tight. "And I turned into an a-hole. I'm so sorry, Angie."

No doubt about it. He was ready to throw in with her. Even at his peril. "I know why you made that speech."

"Because I'm an idiot?"

"Because my brothers asked you to stay away from me."

He went very still. "I don't suppose that's an educated guess."

"Nope."

_11_

Dallas groaned and let his head fall back against the sofa cushion. "Kendall heard me talking to your brother yesterday."

"She did. And I'm glad."

He straightened and turned to face her. "You don't look glad."

"Oh, I hate what they tried to pull on me and I wish you'd told Cheyenne to stuff it, but I understand why you didn't."

Guilt pricked him. "I should have. You and I made a connection back in February. I could see it in your eyes. For the record, I did tell him we had something good going."

"What did he say?"

"That you had a history of brief relationships, here today and gone tomorrow."

She let out a sigh. "And since my interest in you came out of the blue..."

"And now I know why. No wonder you were gunning for him last night. And me. I deserved it."

She cupped his cheek. "I felt like a rat when I walked out of the Buffalo."

"But you came back today. Alone." He studied her. "Is Kendall really exhausted?"

"That's what she told Cheyenne."

"Okay, what's going on? Are you and Kendall—"

"Conspiring to torture my brothers? Yes, we are. When she told me what she'd heard—"

"When was that?"

"On the drive back to my house to fetch the tools. We considered calling a family meeting and exposing this patronizing scheme, but it seemed like we'd be letting them off too easy."

"And you don't want to do that."

She shook her head.

He studied her. "Well, there goes my plan."

"Which was?"

"By the time I came out with the coffee, I'd decided to tell Cheyenne the deal was off, that I don't believe you'll toss me aside, and I don't agree that our age difference is significant."

She lit up — her smile warm and her eyes filled with a glow that stole his breath. "That's beautiful, Dallas. Were you going to tell me?"

"No. That way you wouldn't find out what he and your brothers had been up to. But you did, anyway." He took a breath. "On second thought, since he doesn't know you know, I can still do it."

"And take the consequences?"

"In exchange for having you look at me like that? In a heartbeat. I'll go over there this morning and—"

She cut him off with a kiss that scorched him all the way to his toes. Then she backed away, still wearing that smile that made him feel like he'd won the lottery.

"I'll go now." He started to get up, but she pulled him back.

"Please don't."

"Why not?"

"Because Cheyenne, along with several of my brothers, need to change their attitude. You're not going to accomplish that by telling him he's wrong. He'll just get irritated and decide *you're* wrong."

"Hm."

"Come here." Cupping his face, she kissed him again, slower this time, teasing him by nibbling on his lower lip, her breath sweet and warm. "I love that you're willing to say those things," she murmured. "Please don't. Not now, anyway."

"Yes, ma'am." He surrendered, capturing her irresistible mouth and delving into the rich sensuality of kissing Angie.

Which brought a predictable result. Lack of oxygen and pain below his belt finally made him lift his head. "Angie, I—"

She gulped for air. "Me, too."

"Let's go back to my—"

"But what if someone—"

"Do you hear a truck?"

Her chest heaved. "Yes, damn it." She gave him a quick peck on the lips before standing and tucking in her shirt. "To be continued."

He got to his feet with a soft groan. "Is that a promise?"

"Yes."

"I sure hope you have a plan."

"I do. For now, keep acting like we're on the outs."

"Okay."

Her attention slid to his fly and she smiled. "That won't help. You might want to disappear for a moment."

"Good idea." He made for the hallway while visualizing a cold shower. Walking into his bedroom with its king-sized bed, he ditched the shower image in favor of one featuring Angie stretched out on — damn, back to square one.

Actually a cold shower was a perfect solution. But taking it would also look suspicious as hell. Whichever brother had dropped by would find Angie measuring planks in the kitchen while he showered. At ten in the morning.

For all he knew, Angie's brothers had quickly made up a schedule after Cheyenne had reported that Kendall was AWOL. Clint had claimed the eight-thirty time slot and this guy could be the ten o'clock watch.

Angie was right. Her brothers' overprotective stance was ridiculous and entrenched. As an outsider, he wouldn't make a dent in their rigid thinking. She and Kendall were the ones to tackle it.

But she'd trusted him with insider info. She'd explained why she'd waited to approach him until she'd turned twenty-five. And she'd indicated she had a plan for making love to him.

He couldn't think about that if he had to go out there and pretend to be mad at her. Although he'd never been much of an actor, he'd do his best.

Their visitor turned out to be Gil, who'd put new shoes on Smoky last month. He stood in the kitchen, nodding as Angie explained the source of the leak and the repairs required. He glanced toward the doorway when Dallas walked in. "Tough break, buddy."

"Life happens." He offered his hand and Gil shook it. "Good to see you." Not really. Gil had just added himself to the list of brothers who wanted to meddle in Angie's business. He could be here because of his concern about the damage, but his timing was suspect.

"Cheyenne and I talked about installing a copper line when he bought this fridge, but they're not as flexible. And they're not foolproof, either."

"Personally, I'm ready to go back to basics. Ice-cube trays." He faced Gil, making no attempt to include Angie in the conversation, like an irritated guy might do.

"I get that. Although it's possible you could install a new line and never have another problem."

"True. Although trays would be—"

"Guys, could you move over by the doorway for this chitchat? I need to start measuring and you're in my way." She sounded convincingly annoyed.

"Sure, sis." Gil shot him a look and walked out into the living room, beckoning him to follow. Once they were several steps away, he lowered his voice. "She's still not happy with you."

"Nope." Should he add anything? Maybe. "The feeling's mutual."

"Yeah, well, give it time. You'll get past it. How's Smoky doing with his new shoes?"

"Seems to like 'em just fine."

"Good, good." Gil put his hat on. "Hey, remember we talked about installing a horseshoe door knocker?"

"I do. Never did ask Cheyenne about it, though."

"I did, and he said it's fine with him."

"Great."

"Turns out I had one tucked in a box of unsold craft fair items. Want to take a look?"

"Sure." He squashed the impulse to give Angie a heads-up that he was going outside. They weren't supposed to be speaking. "Let's see what you've got." He followed Gil out to his tan F-250 with its McLintock Metalworks door magnets. "How's business?"

"Crazy. Warmer weather means more tourists visiting our metalworks shop just when our farrier business is picking up."

"When it rains, it pours." Yet Gil had found time to come over and check on the situation here. All these guys needed to take a step back. Way back.

Gil took the doorknocker out of his truck and handed it over. "How's this?"

"Perfect, dude. Exactly what I envisioned. Has Cheyenne seen it?"

"No, but he told me you had your heart set on buying this place and so you can make this kind of minor decision and he'll consult you on the major ones."

How accommodating. Would Cheyenne feel the same if he knew about the recent kiss fest? Probably not. "What do I owe you?"

"Nothing, buddy. I'm happy you like it."

"No, no. You're in business to make a profit." Dallas pulled his wallet out of his back pocket. "You can't go giving away—"

"Yes, I can." Gil backed away, palms up. "And besides, I brought it partly as an excuse, so we could talk in private."

"Oh?" He didn't have to ask about the topic.

"You dodged a bullet, buddy. Big time. Getting involved with Angie, especially if you plan to live here permanently, is a terrible idea."

"I suppose you're referring to the age difference."

"Actually, that doesn't bother me. Maybe because my mom's eight years older than Bret's and my dad."

"No kidding?"

"Yeah, and they get along great."

"Then why didn't they ever— wait, that's none of my business."

"Get married? Bret and I wondered the same thing. Took us until we were older to figure it out. Mom's a thinker, reads a lot, loves a deep discussion. Our dad, not so much." He shrugged. "Basically, it was a physical attraction. Now they're just friends."

"I see."

"Which is what worries me about you getting involved with Angie. Some women, like Mom for example, can be friends with a guy she used to have sex with. Others can't. I'm pretty sure Angie fits in the second category."

"Why?" He had to ask even if he hated the tack Gil was taking.

"All the guys she's dated have been from out of town. She'd bring them around sometimes to parties and stuff. After she broke up with them, we never saw them again."

"Because they were from out of town." Duh.

"True, but I asked about a couple of them. They were nice guys. She'd completely severed the tie. If you two got sexually involved and then broke up, it'd be a big mess."

"You don't know that. We could handle—"

"Really? Are you saying the past three months haven't been awkward?"

"I suppose, but like you said, we'll get past it. Things will smooth out."

"Because you didn't have sex. When you live in a small town, or worse yet, on this ranch, you'll be bumping into each other, reopening the wound. The fallout will last for years. Trust me."

Dallas studied him. "You have some experience with that?"

"Yeah." He sighed. "I promised never to tell anyone. Not even Bret."

"Then don't feel you have to tell me."

"But it'll make my point. And you're not from here."

"Why does that matter?"

"You haven't known these folks all your life. For sure I can't tell Angie. She'd wade in with both feet. Just listen and keep it to yourself, okay?"

"Okay." Sounded like the guy was dying to tell somebody, so might as well be him.

Gil took a deep breath. "Senior ditch day I had sex with a girl in my class. We weren't dating, just friends. Both virgins. Booze was involved. We dared ourselves into doing it. It was awful."

"I'll bet."

"We promised to keep it secret forever. And we've avoided contact ever since, although we see each other in town all the damned time. To make things worse, her older sister's now my brother's fiancée, so Fa—I mean, the younger one, is invited to family events. She always makes an excuse."

"Have you tried talking with her?"

"Once. Didn't work out." Gil clapped him on the shoulder. "You'll mend fences with Angie, maybe during this repair project. Then just stick with friendship. It's the safest path."

"Thanks for the warning." He didn't want to believe Gil was right about Angie. She likely could have stayed friends with those guys if she'd wanted to. And she'd be friends with him if they broke up. Maybe.

12

Gil kept Dallas out there quite a while, no doubt adding more reasons why a relationship with her would be a disaster. She'd spent her time on the phone with her friend John at Miller's lumberyard.

She'd texted him pictures of the damage and the floorboards she was hoping to match. He had nothing in stock, but a break in customer traffic had allowed him to search online. Didn't look good there, either.

As the engine on Gil's truck revved up outside, Dallas came into the kitchen holding a horseshoe doorknocker.

"Looks like my brother brought you a prezzy."

"He did. Wouldn't let me pay for it."

She grinned. "So you're taking bribes, now?"

"Not just any bribe. This is a classy doorknocker."

"Very classy. Wish I had one. I have doorknocker envy."

"I'd give you this one if it wouldn't blow our cover."

"You don't want it?"

"Oh, I do. I asked him about this weeks ago. I meant to get the okay from Cheyenne and kept forgetting to mention it."

"Let me guess. Gil mentioned it to him when they were on the phone this morning inventing ways to bribe your ass."

"Good guess. Gil just happened to find this one tucked away in the shop."

"And luring you out to the truck was a great excuse to get his hooks into you."

"Sure was. He even admitted it."

"Did he give you a talking-to?"

"Yes, ma'am."

She made a face.

"But he doesn't care about the age difference."

"No? Well goody for him."

"Instead he's worried about the fallout if we get sexually involved and it doesn't work out."

"Oh, for pity's sake! Now they're just making stuff up."

"Could be, but maybe we should discuss the—" He paused and cocked his head. "I hear another truck. Do you think he's coming back?"

"Unlikely. I'm betting the noise you hear is the next wave hitting the shore."

"Can't they see how obvious they're being?"

"If they can, they don't care. I'm gonna go see who it is this time."

"Okay. I'll go get some tools so I can put up the doorknocker."

"My toolbox is sitting right there. You're welcome to—"

"But we're not supposed to be playing nice."

"Oh. Good call." Tucking her phone in her pocket, she walked past him into the living room and peered out the front window. A dark red truck swung into the parking area. Beau. Maybe he'd brought Maverick. That little darling would be on her Auntie Angie's side.

But her favorite brother — or the one who used to be her favorite — climbed out alone and tugged on the brim of his hat. She was tempted to stomp out there and blister his ears, but as she'd said to Dallas, arguing with only one of her scheming siblings wouldn't achieve the result she was going for.

She opened the door as he climbed the porch steps. "You're the third visitor we've had this morning. Are you all bored with your lives?"

"Aw, we're just concerned about Cheyenne's house, sis." He flashed his winning smile. "You know how it is. Somebody lands in the manure pile, the rest come running to hose 'em off."

"Oh, I know how it is." Did she ever. She stepped back to let him in.

"Where's Dallas?"

"Fetching his tools." If only she could call out *Dallas, put on your pants! We have company!*

"Why do you need his? Does he have something you don't?"

He certainly does. "He's not getting them for my use. Gil brought him a doorknocker and he wants to put it up." She rolled her eyes. "By himself. With his own tools."

"Ah. Then you two haven't buried the hatchet." Beau was clearly glad about that.

"Not yet." But if her brothers would stop showing up every five minutes, she might ask Dallas to bury something else. "How come you didn't bring Mav? She would've been fascinated to see the cabinets gone and the floor ripped up."

"Exactly why I didn't bring her. She'd want to crawl around in the demolition zone looking for nails to swallow."

"Probably. Although I keep a clean construction site. She'd be okay."

"You won't be seeing her on Saturday mornings for a while. Jess takes her down to the *Sentinel* for job training with Grandpa Andy."

She laughed. "Yeah, right."

"I'm serious! He's teaching her how to type."

"At nine months?"

"What can I say? She has her mother's genes and her father's—"

"Talent for BS. Anyway, since she's not here, you're welcome to crawl around on the kitchen floor and see what treasures you can find. Just don't swallow any nails."

He laughed and nudged back his hat. "Been there, done that." Sauntering into the kitchen, he crouched down and peered at the gap in the floorboards. "Have you talked to John at Miller's?"

"Just did. Matching what's there is gonna be difficult."

"I'm not surprised."

"I asked him to estimate when he could get this size plank in white oak and he said it could be months."

"I talked to Clint and he's having better luck with the wood for the cabinets."

"That makes sense. They're maple."

"Tell you what I'd do about this floor." He rose to his feet. "I'd— hey, there, Dallas. Ready to install that sucker?"

"That's the plan." He walked in, a small toolbox in one hand and the doorknocker in the other. "But what's this I hear about wood not being available?"

"My sis tells me that white oak flooring is in short supply. Could be quite a while before it could get here."

"Hadn't heard that."

Angie gave him a cursory glance. "I didn't get around to telling you." She'd been having too much fun kidding him about the doorknocker-slash-bribe from Gil. "Could be months. And the cabinets can't go in until the floor's done."

"Understood."

"But no problem, right? You said you'll be happy to wash dishes in the bathroom sink, so I guess it doesn't matter."

"Not to me. This repair can take as long as it takes. I'm fine with it." A tell-tale twinkle appeared briefly in his eyes. Then it was gone.

She ducked her head to hide a smile and pretended to study the ripped-out area. "On top of it, there's more damage than I first thought. I'm gonna remove another section this morning to see what's happening with the subfloor."

"I have a suggestion," Beau said, "for what it's worth."

She glanced at him. "Like what?"

"Do what Jess and I did in our kitchen."

"Tile?"

"Why not? Looks almost like wood and you don't have to lose sleep over something leaking all over it. The leak quotient is huge in this area. You've got your laundry room, the sink, the dishwasher, the refrigerator—all just waiting to puddle all over your lovely hardwood."

Dallas nodded. "That's for sure. And with me being gone so much, this could happen again. How long have you had your tile?"

"Angie and Kendall laid it last summer, before Mav was born, so it's been almost a year. A kid who dumps applesauce and sippy cups full of juice won't be your problem, but cleanup's a breeze if you spill stuff. I don't have a heart attack when something splatters everywhere."

"It's a thought. I'll run it past Cheyenne."

"I already did. He said it's your decision."

Angie swallowed the laugh that almost got loose. It was a wonder Cheyenne had a spare second to watch over Kendall considering the texts and phone calls flying back and forth this morning.

"If you want to see what mine looks like, we could run over there now. The sooner you decide, the better, so Angie knows which direction to go."

"Makes sense."

"But we can hang that doorknocker first. I can help you with that."

"Uh, sure. Thanks."

"In fact, we could head to the barn after looking at the tile. I'm sure Smoky and Champion could use a run if you're up for it."

"I, um, yep, sounds good."

Smooth move, big brother. She and Kendall were good at this kind of cat and mouse game, but so were her siblings, especially Beau. She was determined to bring those boys to their knees, but it wouldn't be easy.

For now, she had to stay cool. "Going with tile is an interesting idea, but that might be hard to get, too."

"It could be, but if Dallas likes what Jess and I have, there's a supply of it in Missoula at the tile place where you and I picked up ours. I called them before I came over."

"You've been busy."

"You know me, sis. Anything for family."

Oh, for a cream pie she could smash into his smiling face.

13

Dallas had never aspired to be a double agent. But if that's what it would take to win Angie's heart, he'd channel his inner James Bond.

Beau offered to give him a ride over to his place which neatly put the guy in charge of the outing. Dallas braced himself for another lecture on the perils of getting involved with Angie.

"Whatever you said to her back in February must have been a doozy." Beau switched on his big F-350 engine. "She's gone all honey-badger on you."

"Guess so."

"How did you break the news to her? If you don't mind my asking."

"I told her I appreciated her help locating and transporting Smoky and I thought she was great, but I was looking for someone closer to my age."

"Oooo. You basically said she was too young. I'll bet she was spittin' fireballs."

"Judging from the names she called me, that's an accurate assessment."

Beau chuckled. "She's got a vocabulary when she gets mad."

"Yeah, she does. Impressive."

"She learned it from us. When she was about five, Mom put her in charge of the swear jar and said she could keep the money. She stalked us constantly and if we weren't swearing, she'd annoy us until we cut loose with a few choice words. It was worth paying to get rid of her."

"Ah, yes. The swear jar. We had one, too." Dallas glanced out the window so Beau wouldn't see how that story about Angie tickled him. He'd tease her about it later. Whenever later happened. Maybe tonight? God, he hoped so.

"I know when she was little she enjoyed being the youngest kid in the family. But somewhere around fourth grade she got tired of that label. Ever since then, she's knocked herself out trying to prove she's old enough to do whatever she darn well pleases."

Which she certainly is now. Keeping his mouth shut was a chore. He'd love to argue with this likeable but wrong-headed cowboy who couldn't accept that his little sister had grown up.

"Y'know, psychologically, it makes sense she'd go for someone older like you. She's the only one who doesn't have a dad anymore."

"Hey, I'm not old enough to be her *father.*"

"I know, but you have the know-how of an adult. That appeals to her. You're not a kid."

And neither is Angie. Time to switch topics. "She told me about her dad. Sounds like he was an amazing guy."

"Yep. He hired out as a carpenter, but he could fix anything that broke. Toys, faucets, light switches, you name it. She inherited his talent, for sure."

"That's obvious."

"I think if Gene hadn't died in that rollover, he and Mom might have tied the knot. But we'll never know." He pulled up in front of his cabin. "I promise you're gonna love this floor."

He did. Soon after walking into Beau's kitchen, he was on the phone to Angie, letting her know he'd like to make the switch to tile. Since she had privacy on her end, she could say things he couldn't. And say them in a way guaranteed to drive him crazy.

She lowered her voice to a sexy purr. "Are you gonna help me lay that tile, cowboy?"

He kept his tone brisk. "I'll see."

"It'll be fun. We'll get all hot and sweaty together and then take a long, hot shower. How does that sound?"

"Yeah, okay." He managed to sound irritated instead of aroused.

"And after that long, steamy shower, we'll—"

"Gotta go." He disconnected.

"She was blistering your butt, wasn't she?"

"Yep." He tucked his phone away.

"Good thing I suggested we go riding. Gives you a reason not to be there while she's taking out the rest of the floor."

"Except with Kendall out of commission, she's doing it by herself. I could have helped."

"Trust me, you don't want to offer your assistance when she's on a tear. She'll work out her frustrations with you by ripping up that floor. If you're lucky, she'll be finished and gone by the time we get back."

"Yeah, that would be better." *Not.*

It bugged him that she was stuck with a job he would have been happy — delighted — to share. Yeah, she'd created the situation, or rather Kendall had by faking exhaustion. But he wanted to be there. For many reasons.

Evidently Beau had picked up on his guilt trip. After they'd saddled the horses and headed down the trail, he reopened the subject. "I can tell this repair job has made a tough situation worse, buddy."

Not exactly true. Before he'd had no shot. Now he had one, but it was complicated as hell. "I suppose it does, in a way."

"I didn't mention it before in case you didn't like the tile, but I figured replacing the hardwood might be what drags this out. Putting in tile shortens the amount of time she needs to be in your house. Once it's done, she has nothing more to do until Clint finishes the cabinets."

"Guess so."

"I'm trying to make this as easy on you as possible, so here's my plan. We make this ride short so we have time to drive to Missoula and pick up the tile. Then we convince Angie to wait until Kendall's rested up so she can help lay it. Kendall's a good buffer, right?"

"Right." Kendall, his fellow secret agent.

"That way you don't feel like you have to help. Obviously you've been raised like I have, to get in there and lend a hand. But asking you to work alongside Angie when the two of you are crossways — that's cruel and unusual punishment."

Dallas turned a bark of laughter into a cough and prayed he'd done it well enough to fool Beau.

"Sorry. Didn't mean to crack you up, but I'm glad you can see the humor in the situation. That icemaker leak was Murphy's Law at work."

Or the hand of Fate. He cleared his throat. "I'll admit I was freaked out when I realized Cheyenne would be hiring her. But I'm sure it'll sort itself out."

"I guaran-damn-tee it will." Beau nudged his sorrel gelding into a trot as they reached a wide meadow. "Time to give these ponies a good run. Then we'll get on with business."

Smoky quivered with eagerness. Grabbing his hat, Dallas increased the pressure on the grey's ribs. Smoky leaped forward, matching his stride to Champion's.

The two horses tore across the meadow on a wide, well-worn path created by years of McLintock use. The meadow was beautiful whether Dallas came out by himself or with one of Angie's brothers. But it took two to race and he got a huge kick out of doing that. So did Smoky.

Today, like most days, it was too close to call. Didn't matter. The rush of riding his own horse through a meadow in Montana was its own reward.

He wouldn't be doing it, at least not yet, if Angie hadn't given him a gentle push. He'd thank her for that the next time they were alone.

"I never get tired of that." Beau glanced over at him as they walked the horses back across the meadow. "Thanks for coming out with me. Racing's a blast."

"I love it. Running across this meadow fits my dream of what living here would be like."

"I admire you for moving here all on your own, not knowing a soul. That takes cojones."

"Didn't feel that scary. Felt more like I was coming to the place where I was supposed to be."

"Very cool." Beau fell silent, then took a quick breath. "I've felt that once, the first time I made love to Jess. I didn't pay enough attention, though."

"What do you mean?"

"She was the one for me, but because I was a jackass, I almost lost her. Maverick gave me a second chance to get my head on straight."

"Maverick? Your baby?"

Beau turned to him. "Right, you probably don't get that. You're such a part of the family now that I— anyway, Mav wasn't planned. We were just dating when Jess got pregnant. Condom failure. Long story about that, but we'd broken up by the time she discovered she was PG."

"I hadn't heard any of that. I'm glad it came together for you two. And Maverick. What a cutie."

"Yeah, she's special. Best damn total surprise of my life. I'm so happy the condom failed, but I wouldn't recommend that path."

"I doubt anyone would."

"Mom told us to use condoms but warned us they're not foolproof. You'd better really like the person you have sex with because you could end up parents of a kid."

"Good advice."

"Maybe that's another reason I'm protective of Angie. I can only imagine what Jess went through when she found out she was pregnant. She had no use for me and yet now she was chained to me by a baby. I have nightmares about my little sister going through that."

"What about your brothers? Don't you worry about them?"

"Sure I do. And I get your point. It's bad news for both parties." He shrugged. "It makes no sense for me to be more concerned about Angie. My mother would call it sexist. But...."

"Yep, it's complicated."

<u>14</u>

Angie left a text for Kendall asking her to call when she had a chance. Not surprisingly, the call didn't come until it was time to feed the horses and tuck the chickens into their coop for the night.

"Hey, Kendall, I—"

"Beau did an end run around us. Cheyenne told me about the tile. It's not a bad idea, but—"

"Beau essentially kidnapped Dallas."

"I didn't anticipate that. Sort of made my plan worthless."

"Not completely worthless. We had privacy between Clint leaving and Gil arriving."

"And?"

"He's one hot kisser."

"I *knew* it! I'm telling you, *firefighters*."

"Right? Then add in the cowboy factor and—"

"Preach it, girlfriend!" Kendall laughed. "What else?"

"Not much. Could've been if Gil hadn't shown up."

"Damn."

"But the main thing is we talked and—"

"Before kissing?"

"Between kissing in the kitchen and kissing on the sofa."

"You kissed in two different venues? That's great news!"

"We would've gone for three venues except for Beau's interference. Anyway, between the two kissing sessions I gave Dallas all the info he needs and he's solidly on our side."

"Which is wonderful except Beau's figured out a way to keep you two far apart. For your own good, of course. How much of the hardwood have you pulled out?"

"I'm done. Beau and Dallas will pull in with the load of tile any time now. After I help them unload it, I'll have no excuse to hang around. Even if I could find one, Beau will outwait me."

"So don't. Take your leave."

"Then what? If I come back after Beau's gone, someone will spot my truck, either on the road or parked here. Dallas can't drive to my place, either."

"Angie McLintock, use your noggin. The road between his place and yours is a big curve. His place is a ways if you take the road, but if you cut through the trees behind the cabins, it's—"

"A five-minute walk!"

"There you go. You don't need a truck to get to Cheyenne's cabin."

"You're right. I can't believe I was focused on driving here."

"Understandable. You're on hormone overload."

"I don't want to scare the wits out of him by just appearing."

"He'll get over it."

"Yeah, but maybe I need to text him once I'm halfway there. Not before, though. He'd try to meet me and get lost in the trees."

"Speaking of phones, don't bother texting me regarding your activities. This is a done deal and I have a vivid imagination."

"I wasn't planning to text you. I'll be too busy."

"Don't wear yourself out, though. I'm coming with you to lay tile tomorrow and I expect you to pull your weight."

"Didn't you hear? I'm supposed to take tomorrow off and we'll do the tile when you're recovered."

"I'll just recover faster than expected. I see no point in lying around here when there's plotting to be done. If I'm over there working with you and Dallas, the boys will leave us alone and we can plan our next moves."

"Won't you get pushback from Cheyenne?"

She laughed. "He might try, but he learned early on that he's not the boss of me."

"Smart man. Well, I hear Beau's truck pulling in, so I—"

"Don't forget to skedaddle home at daybreak so you can change and meet me back over there at nine."

"What if Cheyenne wants to come with you?"

"I'll find something urgent he needs to do here at home. Some task that can't wait."

"Okay, gotta go." She disconnected right as the door opened and Dallas walked in.

His gaze met hers for a split second but it was enough to send a potent message filled with longing and frustration.

Too bad she couldn't tell him she'd come up with a plan, or rather Kendall had. Instead she looked past him to Beau, who wore his typical jaunty smile.

"Hey, sis. Thought we'd better check to see how you've done before we bring anything more in here."

"All finished." She swept a hand toward the kitchen. "Since the boards could still be used for something, I stacked them in the second bedroom."

Beau strolled into the kitchen and let out a whistle of approval. "Nice."

"I skipped the laundry room for now. Once the kitchen has time to set, we can pull out the washer and dryer and tile that section and the spot under the fridge." She glanced over her shoulder at Dallas. "You might want to do your laundry tonight." And then he could do her.

"Um, okay."

"I thought we were waiting until Kendall's up to it." Beau looked at her, eyebrows raised.

His use of *we* confirmed her suspicion. He'd taken charge of this operation, both the repairs and the meddling. Normally Sky organized the troops. Could it be he wasn't part of this?

In any case, Beau wasn't as firmly in control as he imagined. "I just talked to Kendall and she's rested up. She wants to dive into this project in the morning and get 'er done. Unless Dallas objects, we'll start at nine tomorrow."

"I have no objection."

"Alrighty, then." Beau looked pleased with the turn of events. "We'd best haul in that tile. Dallas, when do you go back on duty?"

"Tuesday morning."

"I predict they'll have that tile laid before you leave. Not grouted, of course, but finished enough that you can see how it's gonna look."

No doubt about it. Beau had appointed himself the campaign field marshal. He likely believed he was saving her from this awkward situation. Because he loved her. She loved him, too, but she still wanted to wring his neck.

He'd remembered to bring his hand truck, so transporting the tile and mortar from the back of his truck into the house didn't take long. But he lingered, continuing to chat with Dallas about the advantages of tile, the luck they'd had because it happened to be on sale, Maverick's problems with teething... blah, blah, blah.

She was tempted to annoy him by hanging around, but that wouldn't fit the scenario she was projecting. She wanted Beau to think she couldn't wait to get away from Dallas.

Walking over to the coat tree, she plucked her denim jacket off one of the hooks. "So long, guys. It's been a long day and I'm ready for a hot shower and some din-din."

Beau looked relieved. "Have a good night, sis."

"Thanks, Beau. You, too." She was counting on her night being way better than his, especially if Maverick was going through another teething phase.

Her truck's tires kicked up a little dust driving home. She would spend the night cradled in Dallas's strong arms. She'd finally make love to the man who'd captured her heart — and her hoo-ha — from the moment she'd caught a glimpse of him on the stage at the Buffalo.

Although she was quivering with anticipation, she took her time in the shower. She'd waited more than a year for this moment. She would arrive for their secret rendezvous with her skin soft, silky and fragrant with the peppermint scent Dallas was fond of.

She dressed in her sexiest pajamas, a white satin tank top and shorts. Then she pulled on her snow boots because they were cushy inside and she didn't want to bother with socks. Fluffing out her freshly washed hair, she put on a parka to ward off the chill and picked up her phone.

A text from Dallas? She opened it. *Beau's gone. I'm on my way.*

On his way? He'd sent it five minutes ago, while she was still getting ready. She rushed to the front window. No truck.

Had he broken down in the short distance from his house to hers? And why was he taking the chance of driving over here?

Might as well text him back. *Where are you?*

A soft rap on the back door had her flying through the kitchen to open it.

He stood on the steps, the kitchen light caressing every inch of his six-foot-two, broad-chested wonderfulness. He thumbed back his Stetson and smiled. "Howdy."

Giddy laughter poured out of her. "You're here!"

"Yes, ma'am."

"Where's your truck?" She peered around him to the yard beyond.

"I walked."

"But you don't know the way!"

"Of course I know the way." He held up his phone. "GPS. Can I come in?"

<u>15</u>

Angie moved back, still giggling. And breathless. That was a good sign. Dallas was a little short of air, too. Technically he hadn't jogged over here, but the term *race walk* might apply.

Heart galloping like a mustang, he stepped inside. She kept looking at him like she couldn't believe her eyes. "Did you think I'd just sit over there in my house now that you've told me how things are?"

"I guess I did."

"Then you don't know me very well."

"I hope that's about to change."

"I believe it will." She was so close. So fragrant. And so strangely dressed. "Why are you wearing a parka and snow boots?"

"To keep me warm while I walked to your cabin."

"Seriously?" That sure was good for the ego.

"Great minds. Want to give me your jacket?"

"Absolutely." He shrugged out of it and tucked his phone in the front pocket. Then he handed over his hat, too.

She hooked both on pegs by the door before facing him. Her blue eyes had the same gleam they'd had this morning. He could stare into them forever. Or maybe not. Now that he was standing inches away from her, his body was making demands. "Gonna keep that parka on?"

"Would you like me to take it off?"

"Yes, ma'am."

Maintaining eye contact, she unzipped it slowly, peeled it off her shoulders and let it drop to the floor.

"Damn." He swallowed. "That's enough to drive a man crazy."

Her voice took on the sultry sound she'd used on the phone. "Just what I was going for." She glanced down at his boots. "Might as well take those off so you won't track dirt through the house."

He toed them off. "Good idea." Clearly they'd be heading for her bedroom any minute, but he was old-fashioned enough to want an invite.

"I'm loaded with ideas."

"I wonder if they're anything like my ideas?"

"One way to find out." She twirled around and started off, her dark hair loose and bouncing against her shoulders. "Follow me."

"You bet."

She led him through the kitchen and flipped off the light on her way out. The rapid thump of her snow boots on the hardwood should have been funny.

But those black rubber boots paired with white satin that clung to her pert breasts and her sweet tush was the sexiest combo he'd ever seen. As they passed through her living room, he had no interest in looking around. The view straight ahead claimed all his attention. "Why snow boots?"

"Because they don't require socks."

He got the picture. Socks took time. She'd be naked in five seconds. Heat romped through his body and gathered below his belt. It was a wonder he could walk. "I'm overdressed."

"I'll take care of that."

Now he couldn't breathe, either. And he was sweating. He popped the snaps on his cuffs.

She glanced over her shoulder. "Getting a head start?"

"Just trying to help out." He left his shirt in the hallway, grabbed the back of his T-shirt, yanked it over his head and dropped it, too.

He'd unbuckled his belt by the time she disappeared into a dark room near the end of the hall. He followed her in and paused so he wouldn't run her down.

"Hang on." Something hit the floor. Twice.

When she switched on a lamp, her back was to him and she was barefoot. Her skimpy satin outfit remained the only barrier between him and total immersion in the wonder that was Angelique McLintock. He was ready to explode.

She turned around, her chest rising and falling as rapidly as his. Her eyes widened and she sucked in a breath.

"Something wrong?"

"Oh, no." Her cheeks flushed. "Something is very, very right."

He couldn't say who moved first, but the next second she was plastered against him and he was kissing her for all he was worth. He had to stop for two seconds so he could pull her tank top over her head.

Then he was back, plunging his tongue into her hot mouth, cupping her silken breasts and stroking his thumb over her taut nipples. The buzz of his zipper made him groan in anticipation.

No stopping. Not this time. When she shoved at the waistband of his jeans, the weight of his belt took them to the floor. He extricated his feet and nudged the jeans away.

When he hooked his thumbs in the waist of her shorts, slid them past her hips and let them fall, she pushed down his briefs. Next thing he knew she'd wrapped her fingers around his cock. Game over. Ending the kiss, he gazed into eyes the color of deep twilight. No question what she was after, and she wasn't shy about it.

He had the shakes and his throat felt like sandpaper. "Better turn me loose so I can fetch a condom."

"Meet you in bed."

Stepping out of his briefs, he picked up his jeans and plucked out one of the foil squares.

"Who did you buy those for?"

Odd question. "Me." He ripped open the package.

"I mean... were you expecting... to have sex with a certain... someone?" Her rapid breathing punctuated the question with little gasps.

"Yes." Once the condom was on, he glanced up. His brain stalled.

She lay on her side, head propped on her hand, watching him. With all her glorious, wild hair and her lithe, perfect body, she could be a goddess who'd chosen to take a mortal as her lover. How could he be this lucky?

"You don't have to tell me." She scooted over to make room as he approached the bed. "That was a nosy—"

"It was you." He slipped in beside her and gathered her close.

"Me?"

"You." He rolled her to her back and moved between her thighs. "You're the one that I want."

"Ditto." She wrapped her arms around him. "Come get me."

"Yes, ma'am." He held her gaze and pushed deep. "We'll take it easy the first—" He gasped as she tightened around him.

"I don't think so, cowboy." She dug her fingertips into his glutes. "It's gonna be a wild ride."

Just like that, his body hijacked his brain. "*Hell*, yeah." He went a little crazy and she urged him on, panting and calling for more, more, *more*.

He gave her all he had and then some. When she came, she yelled loud enough to make his ears ring. And they kept on ringing as his climax arrived like the grand finale at the Fourth of July fireworks show.

When the spasms eased, and he had enough air in his lungs to keep from passing out, he opened his eyes and looked down. "I'm dripping sweat on you."

She smiled. "I like that in a man. Shows you really got into it."

"You noticed that, huh?"

"Did you really think we'd have polite sex?"

"Until today I didn't think we'd ever have sex, polite or otherwise."

"You must've thought we would or you wouldn't have bought those condoms."

"Okay, for about twenty-four hours, when we were involved in the whole Smoky deal, before Cheyenne took me aside, I was pretty sure we were going to have sex. That's when I bought the condoms."

"I thought we were, too. Which is why your little speech made me so mad. I should have figured out it wasn't in character, though."

"How? You didn't really know me. I didn't really know you."

"But we just took a crash course in all things us. I can't speak for you, but I'd say we learned a lot."

That made him smile. "Like what?"

"You were really loud there at the end."

"Oh, and you weren't? My ears are still ringing."

She blinked. "Whoops. That's not your ears. It's Kendall's ringtone. My phone's in the kitchen. I need to—"

"I'll vamoose." He eased away from her and left the bed. "Pillow talk to be continued." He walked into the attached bath, disposed of the condom and washed up.

What a beginning they'd had. Judging from this first round, they—

"*Dallas.*" Angie rushed in, her robe half on and half off, her arms full of his clothes, including his hat, jacket, and the shirts he'd left on his way to the bedroom. "Cheyenne's on his way here."

"What? Why would he—"

"I'll explain later. Take these and hide while I pull on some clothes and make the bed."

"Hide? Where?"

"I don't know." She jerked open a drawer and pulled out sweatpants and a sweatshirt. "Where do people hide in a situation like this?"

"How should I know? I've never been in a—"

"The closet! Get in there." She wiggled into sweatpants and pulled a sweatshirt over her head. "Don't make any noise and don't come out until I come get you."

"What about my boots? I left them—"

"I stuck them outside on my back porch. In the closet. *Now.*"

"Want me to make the bed, first?"

"No! Just get in there! I hear his truck coming up the road."

"Yes, ma'am." He snagged his jeans and opened her bi-fold closet doors. "I won't fit."

"Just shove some clothes aside." She straightened the comforter and stacked the pillows against the headboard.

"I don't know how I'll get it closed from the inside."

"I'll do it."

Bunching her clothes at one end on the rod, he created enough space once he shoved her collection of boots aside. But he'd have to sit on the floor. He pulled his jacket out of the mix and tossed it down to cushion his bare butt. "Okay, I'm in."

She hurried over and started to giggle.

"Hey."

"Sorry, but you look—"

"Ridiculous? Close the damned door, okay?"

"I'll get rid of him as soon as I can. Sorry about this." She was still grinning when she closed the folding door.

It was louvered so he wasn't in complete darkness. The bedside lamp was still on, so— nope, she switched that off. Dark as the inside of a campground privy. Smelled better, though.

<u>16</u>

Angie grabbed a scrunchie from the bathroom before dashing out the door of her bedroom. On the way down the hall, she gathered her hair into a ponytail.

She hadn't put on makeup for the walk over to Dallas's place. A good thing, because if Cheyenne saw makeup on her when she was supposedly hanging out at home by herself, he'd be suspicious.

She should be doing something when he arrived. Like what? Oh, yes, cooking dinner! Or better yet, warming up leftovers. She opened the fridge and scanned the contents. No leftovers.

Was Dallas hungry? No doubt. Her stomach was starting to growl. Once she got rid of Cheyenne she'd consult with Dallas and see what they might whip up together. Other than another spectacular roll in the hay, of course.

Her lady parts tingled. She'd been right about him. About them. About how well they fit together. In so many delicious ways.

Why had she been convinced they would? It was a mystery. In fact, she couldn't claim credit, really. Some deeply buried instinct had—

Cheyenne rapped on the door, a quiet, unobtrusive knock. Such a sweet, peaceful guy. And such a royal pain in the ass.

She went to the door and opened it. "Hey, there! What brings you to my door?"

He came in and took off his hat. "Sorry to bother you, but I tried calling and you didn't answer. Then I tried calling Dallas and he didn't answer, and I—"

"Call about what?" Kendall had already told her, but he didn't know that.

And by the way, where had Dallas put his phone after he'd walked into her house? Oh, yeah, in his jacket pocket. Fingers crossed nobody called him since he might not remember to silence it.

"Kendall told me about the plan to do the kitchen floor tomorrow, then pull the washer and dryer out once the floor's set and do the laundry room."

"That's what we decided."

"She says she's fine, all rested up, but you know me. I worry."

"I do know you." Far better than you think, big brother.

"So instead, how about if you pull the washer and dryer out tomorrow, take up that floor and tile it?"

"Why?"

"It would be a smaller job. And you can push the bigger job to a later date when we can be sure Kendall's up to it."

"Hard to argue with your reasoning." And she wouldn't, because that would take more time. "Let's do it that way."

"Good. I'm glad you agree. I figured you'd go along with it once you heard my reasoning. Kendall says I'm overreacting and she's just fine, but—"

"You're allowed to overreact a little. You've never had a baby before."

"I wish I could have this baby. Literally go through labor and delivery for Kendall. Beau feels the same about Jess. Sky said something similar about Penny."

"But that's not how Mother Nature set it up."

He grimaced. "Unfortunately. Have you felt the baby kick?"

"Several times."

"Isn't that cool? It's getting to the point where I hate to go on duty, because I'm missing stuff. She sings to our baby and when I'm home, so do I, even though I'm a little off key. I love my job, but—"

"And the paycheck."

"Yeah, there's that. And babies cost money, and after all, it is the job I've wanted ever since—"

"Since you were eight years old. I know. Listen, I don't want to be rude, but I'm starving and I need to start cooking dinner."

"Oh! Sure. I'll be on my way." He put on his hat and tugged on the brim. "So why didn't you answer?"

"Must have been in the shower."

"Then Dallas didn't answer, either."

"I guess he could have been in the shower, too."

"Maybe. It was weird, though. I knew you and Dallas were at home and yet I couldn't get either of you."

"Just one of those crazy coinkidinks."

"Weird, though." He pulled out his phone. "I'll just call him now and explain the change of plans."

She slapped her hand over his phone. "Don't."

He gave her a look. "Why not? He needs to know what—"

"No, he doesn't."

"But his washer and dryer will be out of commission for a couple of days and we go back on duty on—"

"I told him to do his laundry tonight just to be on the safe side."

"Yeah, okay, but—"

"It would be very inconsiderate to call him at this hour."

"It's not even eight o'clock."

"He was frazzled when I left. Not that I care about his mental state, but I think this whole thing has been tough on him. I wouldn't be surprised if he took a shower, grabbed a sandwich and went straight to bed." How she said it without laughing was a minor miracle.

Cheyenne frowned. "I don't see him as being that fragile, Ang. I mean, the guy marches straight into burning buildings. He moved cross-country, alone, to a place where he had no friends or family, and made a home for himself. A leaking ice maker hose isn't—"

"He's fallen in love with that house. Take my word for it. He was frazzled. Leave him be."

"Okay, if you say so." He shrugged. "But if you're right, he isn't doing his laundry, either. When Tuesday comes he'll be SOL."

She hadn't thought of that. "If he hasn't done it, I'm sure you and Kendall will let him come over and use your washer and dryer."

"Of course we will. Alrighty, you've convinced me." He touched two fingers to the brim of his hat. "I'm outta here."

"See you later, big brother."

"Yeah, I'll probably come by and check on you and Kendall tomorrow."

"Great." Just wonderful.

He started out the door and turned back. "Come to think of it, I sort of explained the change in plans when I left him a message. I hope he's okay with it."

"Trust me, he won't mind at all." She walked over and took hold of the door.

"Hope not. I like the guy. I want him to be happy." He gave her a smile. "Now I'm really leaving."

"Bye." She closed the door and stood by it until she heard the rumble of his truck's engine. Then she twisted the lock and ran back to her bedroom. "He's gone!"

"Thank the Lord!"

"Wow, I have a talking closet!" She flung open the doors. Dallas sat cross-legged wearing his Stetson, his T-shirt, and nothing else. She cracked up. "Sorry, sorry, sorry."

"Having fun?"

"Why…" She gulped back laughter. "Why put on just that?"

Setting his pile of clothes outside the closet, he got to his feet. "It was all I could manage in a small space. I figured if the worst came, I'd get out… somehow, and quickly pull on my jeans."

"Why bother with your hat?"

He tugged on the brim. "It gives me gravitas."

"Do tell?"

"You don't think so?"

"Now that you mention it, yes, I do. It also ramps up your sexy quotient."

"Aha." He stepped closer. "You like me in this hat."

"Heck, yeah." Warmth sluiced through her.

"Ever done it with a Stetson-wearing man?"

"Can't say that I have."

"Then let's fix that." He scooped her up in his arms.

"Hey, I can walk over there, Stetson-man!"

"Be quiet." He deposited her on top of the quilt. "I'm showing off my bulging firefighter muscles."

He could deposit her anywhere he liked as long as he followed up with some stellar lovemaking. "Are we talking about the muscles that get my panties wet?"

"They would if you were wearing panties." He neatly stripped off her sweatpants. "But you're not. Conveniently." He tossed them aside and took hold of her sweatshirt hem. "Put your arms over your head."

"Bossy, much?"

"I prefer *masterful*. It goes with the hat."

"Okay, then." She lifted her arms.

He pulled her sweatshirt over her head and flung it away. Then he gently lifted her head, removed the scrunchie and laid her head back on the pillow. "There. That's better."

"Better for what?"

"You're about to find out. First I have to sheath my manly sword."

She grinned. "Where did you get that description?"

"From a book." Walking back to his pile of clothes, he picked up his jeans and shoved his hand in a front pocket. "More romantic, don't you think?"

Romantic. She liked hearing that word on his lips. Liked it a lot. "Yes, definitely."

He suited up and returned to the bed. "Our first time wasn't very romantic." Climbing in, he moved over her and braced himself on his forearms.

"Fun, though."

"Sure was. But I didn't tell you that you looked like a goddess lying there. I thought it, but I didn't say so."

"A goddess? Really?"

His gaze held hers. "Really. I couldn't believe I was about to make love to you. You're perfect, Angelique. Stunning."

Her breath caught. Men had said such things to her, using flattery to coax her into bed. Their words had been empty and meaningless. A total turnoff.

But she'd already welcomed Dallas into her bed. He didn't need to say pretty things to get what he wanted. Clearly he meant every word. He was speaking from his heart. And he was melting hers.

She cupped his face, her palms touching the prickly beginnings of a beard he'd likely shave off in the morning. He'd be in his cabin, then, because he couldn't stay past dawn.

And she wanted him to. She wanted days and weeks with him to explore the wonderful adventure they'd begun. She had to bring this charade to an end soon. Very soon.

_17_

Dallas sure liked the tender way Angie was looking at him right now. It boded well for the future. Their future.

Earlier this year he'd built some castles in the sky — ranches, really — and then had to bomb them to bits. Today they'd risen from the ashes.

And tonight... holding her gaze, he shifted position, probed gently and pushed deep. Her gasp of pleasure fired his blood. "Feel good?"

"You know it." She arched her back. "Lean down more. Tickle me with that manly chest hair."

"Yes, ma'am. Happy to." He sank lower and made contact with her taut nipples. "Like that?"

Her breath quickened. "Just like that."

Easing back, he rocked forward. And again. And once more, setting up a steady rhythm that stroked her breasts and her warm channel with each thrust of his hips. When he focused on the luminescent blue of her eyes, he found all the inspiration he needed for building dreams.

She rose to meet him each time. A slight quiver ran through her body when they briefly formed that tight connection. He grew hungry for that connection, pushing with more force, striking the match that made sparks flare in her eyes.

Her kiss-reddened lips parted. So tempting. The next time he rocked forward he paused long enough to dip his head and touch down. With his cock up to the hilt in her snug chamber, he made love to her mouth.

And she made love to his — nibbling, licking, exploring, capturing his tongue, letting him suck on hers. The first spasm of her climax jolted him, catching him off guard. He'd made her come just by kissing?

Lifting his head, he looked down at her as another spasm gave him an intimate squeeze. "Angie?"

"Uh-huh." She gulped. "It's happening."

He fought his natural response, but it was too late. Her cries of pleasure combined with wave after wave rolling over his cock blasted through his control. He let go with a groan of surrender.

Closing his eyes, he gasped for breath as his steady pulses blended with hers. Last time had been a rocket ship ride. This was far more intimate.

Locked in tight for the whole show, they'd shared as much of the experience as humanly possible. And he liked it.

Her breathing slowed and she let out a sigh of contentment. "Nice."

"Uh-huh."

"Hey, are you hungry?"

He opened his eyes, looked down at her and smiled. His cock was happy enough to blot out anything else going on in his body. "Are you?"

"Starving." She stroked his back. "But before we get some food, I just want to say that was sexy and unusual and I wouldn't mind doing it again some time."

He laughed. "Me, too. I didn't mean it to turn out that way. I just felt like kissing you."

"Well, I certainly didn't expect to react like I did. But it was special." She reached up and stroked his cheek. "Thank you."

"I'll bet the hat had something to do with you coming so quick."

"Maybe. I liked seeing it on you. But when you started kissing me, I forgot all about your hat, or being hungry. Now I'm hungry again."

"Did you even eat today? I should have thought of that. I ran off with Beau and left you to fend for yourself. Some guy I am."

"You're some guy, all right. Some wonderful guy."

"But I—"

"Just because I'm working on your house doesn't mean you're responsible for feeding me. I brought my lunch with me like I usually do."

"Not the first day, though. Marybeth put on a feast."

"Well, sure. But that was a crisis situation and she wanted to check out the damage. She also has a lovely habit of bringing food whenever she comes to anyone's house."

He chuckled. "I'll invite her more often."

"Unfortunately, she hasn't been to my place recently. I meant to go shopping this weekend and didn't. We'll have to scrounge a little."

"For the chance to spend the night with you, I'd eat peanut butter and jelly."

"You might have to." She ran a finger over his lips. "You'll also need to move or we'll starve to death right here."

"See, that's the problem. I like it right here."

"We can eat dinner and come back, you know."

"You say that, but we've already had one surprise visitor. What did he want, anyway?"

"I'll tell you over dinner."

"Okay, I can take a hint." His regret was real as he left her for the necessary trip to dispose of the condom. With the threat of an interruption always hanging over their heads, he wouldn't take any of their private moments for granted.

When he returned, she'd left the bedroom and her sweats and sweatshirt were gone. The sound of pans clattering and the refrigerator door opening and closing told him she was getting a start on their dinner.

Silly as it sounded, he wished he'd asked her to wait for him. He dressed quickly, eager to see her again. No point in putting on his long-sleeved shirt.

Or his hat. He didn't want her to think he was angling for sex all the time. He wasn't, even though he'd never turn down an opportunity. Spending the night here wasn't all about the physical aspect. He wanted to be with her, get to know her better.

As he zipped his jeans, the remaining condom packages in his pocket crinkled. He debated for a few seconds and finally took them out and laid them on the bedside table.

Before walking over to her cabin he'd spent way too much time wondering how many to bring. More than two, less than six. He'd settled on five. Better to have too many than not enough.

Now that he wasn't blinded by lust, he took a quick survey of the room — a queen sleigh bed in a rich walnut, nightstands and dresser in the same wood, the infamous closet, and an entire wall of bookshelves.

So many books, plus a worn teddy bear, several Breyer horses, and framed snapshots of her family. Near the bookshelves, a floor lamp stood sentry next to a cozy chair with a footstool.

Was he the first lover she'd invited in here? Probably not. Except her brothers had made a point of saying her boyfriends had all been from out-of-town. He was the outlier.

Then again, she'd intended for them to have sex at his place. He'd preempted her plan. Maybe she would have preferred that. And now he wanted to know.

He walked quickly through the living room, which also featured a lot of walnut. Must be her favorite. He liked it, too. He'd grown up with sturdy walnut furniture.

When he stepped into the kitchen, she was peering inside the refrigerator. "Looking for something?"

"Something that isn't here. Something that doesn't look like breakfast."

"Nothing wrong with breakfast. I eat it every day."

She sighed and closed the door. "The truth is, I'm not much of a cook. I love to eat, but I'm not into the creative part. I'd ten times rather fix a leaky faucet than a meal."

"Lucky for you, I like to cook."

She blinked. "You do? Oh, that's right. Firefighter. Cheyenne had to brush up on his skills when he hired on."

"Why don't I see what I can do with what you've got?"

"Oooo, baby, c'mon over." She spread her arms wide.

He grinned. "Don't say it if you don't mean it."

"Most of me means it. My tummy is yelling *feed me, girl.*"

"Then step aside. I need room to work."

She moved away from the refrigerator. "It's all yours, but I warn you, everything in there is boring as hell."

"We'll see about that." He opened the door and took inventory. "I'll need a baking dish, a frying pan and a bowl for mixing the eggs. Oh, and a cutting board and a sharp knife." He pulled out a carton of eggs. She only had seven, but that would do.

"The frying pan's on the stove. I'll get out the rest."

"I'm happy to make the meal but I'll let you be in charge of drinks." Laying the eggs on the counter, he scooped up three lonely potatoes and half an onion and some wilted spinach, the only contents of her crisper drawer.

"Will it taste like breakfast?"

"Yes, ma'am." A jar of salsa sat on a shelf. He grabbed it and set it on the counter, too.

"Then I guess we shouldn't have beer."

"Is there a law against it?" He closed the refrigerator door and turned around.

"No." She gazed at him. "I've just never had beer with breakfast."

"Neither have I, but since this is technically dinner—"

"You're right. We're coloring outside the lines anyway, so why not have beer with—" She gestured toward the food on the counter. "Whatever this turns out to be."

"Attagirl."

"Can I do anything to help?"

"You can hang around and talk to me." He moved everything closer to the sink and started washing the potatoes. "Nice cutting board, by the way."

"Clint made that in shop his junior year. He's made a bunch since then, but I like that one because it was his first, the start of his passion for woodworking."

"He's talented, all right." He admired the guy, but not his stance regarding Angie. "I have a really nosy question for you." He started chopping potatoes. "Feel free to tell me it's none of my business."

"All right. What's the question?"

He kept chopping. "Am I the first guy who's been in your bedroom?"

"No, of course not."

His chest tightened. Not what he wanted to hear. He grabbed the onion and chopped faster.

"I'm pretty sure all my brothers have been in there one time or another. I had a lot of help getting moved in, and—"

"I didn't mean like that." He stopped before he pulverized the onion. "I meant—"

"Oh, you want to know if I've had sex with anyone in there besides you! Why didn't you say so?"

He glanced over at her, his breathing not as steady as he would have liked. "I thought I did."

"No, you didn't. You asked if you were the first guy I'd had in there. Which I thought was an odd question. You know I'm surrounded by—"

"So am I the first or not?"

She met his gaze. "Yes, you are."

"Is that because I barged over here? Would you rather have been at my place?"

"Not at all. Except you might have better food in your fridge."

"Then you're fine with having me in your bedroom?"

"More than fine. Why are you asking?"

"Because it seems significant."

She lit up, as if he'd just said something brilliant. Her eyes grew bright. "That's because it is."

His world tilted. Was she serious about this relationship? Hell, yeah. Far from being impulsive and scattered about her love life, she'd managed it with the skill of a five-star general. And she'd chosen him.

_18_

"Did I freak you out?" Angie peered at Dallas. He'd gone completely still except for his eyes. They'd registered shock at first and then a whole parade of intense emotions in rapid succession, as if he was on overload.

"I—" He stopped to clear his throat. "I wouldn't say that, exactly." He laid the knife on the cutting board and wiped his hands on a dishtowel. "_Honored_ might be a better description of how I feel." He turned and gave her a crooked smile. "Might be a little bit of intimidation mixed in there, too."

"Oh, Dallas." She closed the distance and wrapped her arms around him, giving him a hug. "Are you worried I've put you on a pedestal?"

He hugged her back. "God, I hope not, but if I'm the first guy you've let into your bedroom, you must think I'm a cut above the average."

Lifting her face to his, she smiled. "Well, you are all that and more or I wouldn't have invited you there in the first place, but here's the deal. Your timing is excellent."

"How so?"

"You moved to the ranch after I'd been in business a year and I'd just taken on Kendall as my assistant. I was settled in my own house and I was only ten months from my twenty-fifth birthday. I was primed for the next step."

He tensed. "The next step being...."

"My first serious relationship." She felt his muscles relax a little. "Did you think I meant marriage?"

"Not exactly, but I—"

"So you did. No wonder you got all tense when I said *next step*. That's not a *next step*. It's a flying leap, which would be insane since we barely know each other."

"Because your brothers stifled your plans."

"Yep. I had it mapped out. I'd flirt with you at my b-day party, and if that went well, I'd see about getting you a horse. Then we could start riding together and let the chips fall."

"What if I'd refused to get a horse?"

"It might not have been a deal breaker, but I would have questioned whether I wanted to be with someone who wasn't open to having his own horse. But you did want Smoky. And you love him, right?"

"Yes, ma'am. Even when he was trying to take a piece out of me, and now we've come to an understanding about that. When I was out riding with Beau today I reminded myself to thank you for pushing me to get Smoky."

"Just a gentle nudge."

He smiled. "More like a forceful shove, but I'm not complaining."

She hugged him tighter. "You feel a lot more relaxed, now. Do you believe me when I say I'm not focused on a trip down the aisle?"

"Not at all?" He sounded disappointed.

"Oh, I'd like to someday, and in time, you and I might decide that's the right move for us." She studied him. "Unless you have something against the idea. If so, tell me now."

"Because it's a deal breaker?"

Anxiety twisted in her stomach. She hadn't considered he might be marriage phobic, but he was thirty-two, so maybe—

"Didn't mean to scare you. I'm in favor of marriage, especially if kids will be involved and I'd like to have kids, too, in case you're wondering."

She let out a breath. "Good, because if you'd turned out to be a confirmed bachelor or you never wanted kids, I'd have to kick you out right now."

"Before I cooked this meal?"

She grinned. "Good point. I'm so hungry I might keep you around long enough for that. But no hanky-panky after dinner. I used to be able to have sex even if I knew the relationship wasn't going anywhere. Those days are over."

He cupped her face in one hand and leaned down. "They're over for me, too." Then he kissed her, a sweet, undemanding touch of his lips before lifting his head. "Time for me to start cooking."

"Yes, please." She let go of him, but his words stayed with her. *They're over for me, too.* Hallelujah, they were on the same page, hoping for something special, wanting to make sure they didn't move too fast. So far, her instincts had served her well.

He went back to preparing the meal while she related Cheyenne's suggested change for tomorrow's tile-laying project.

"That's fine with me." He put the baking dish in the oven.

"He was worried you wouldn't do your laundry tonight."

"Now that's a valid concern. There's zero chance I'll spend any part of this night on laundry."

"Is that a problem? Do you need clean clothes for starting work on Tuesday?"

"Yes, but I guarantee any one of your brothers will offer to help me with that, provided they don't find out I spent the night with their little sis."

"I don't think they will. Not until you and I tell them."

"About that. I have questions." He checked the time on her kitchen clock. "Potatoes will take about thirty minutes and I don't want to start the omelet yet. Let's grab those beers and go sit in your living room."

"Works for me." Opening the fridge, she took out two bottles. "We could eat in there if you want. I've set it up so you can see the fireplace from the table. But of course I don't have a fire going."

"Oh, yes, you do."

"In the *fireplace.*" She handed him one of the bottles.

"Just sayin'." He tapped his bottle against hers. "Here's to keeping the flame alive."

"Are you sure we're going in there to chat?"

"Scout's honor. I have it on good authority you're starving and if we burn those potatoes, you have no Plan B. If I could get away with it, I'd give you some stuff from my fridge to tide you over."

"Having to keep our relationship on the down-low sucks." She led the way into the living room.

"Yes, it does, which is why I'd like to bring an end to that as soon as we can reasonably manage it." He paused, surveying the room. "This is a great arrangement."

"I like it. By putting the fireplace on the kitchen wall and a bay window on the opposite wall, my dining table has a view of the mountains and the fireplace."

"And you raised the hearth so you'll see that fire, even though there's a sofa in front of it. Good planning."

"All my brothers went for an eat-in kitchen like yours, but I wanted a living-dining room combo. The round table's nice for two, but I have two leaves that turn it into a good-sized oval."

"Nice."

"This is my favorite part." She reached for the wall switch and turned on the graceful wrought-iron chandelier hanging above it. "Bret and Gil made me this last year."

"Wow. That's impressive." He walked over and examined it. "Beautiful work. It's just the right size for that space."

"Bret made a rough sketch first to guarantee it was what I had in mind."

"Your brothers clearly adore you."

"And I adore them. But they also drive me nuts."

He smiled. "I know. Anyway, it seems like we should make a fire and take advantage of this great setup, but you'd have to tend it while I fix the eggs."

"Happy to. Let's get this baby blazing." She walked over to the hearth, set down her beer and reached for the gloves on top of the wood rack.

"Would you let me do it?"

She glanced at him. "You really want to?"

"I do. You worked so hard today while I went on a great ride and took a trip to Missoula. Makes me want to do things for you."

She smiled. "You have."

"Other things."

"Then be my guest." She picked up her beer. "I'll sit on the sofa and relax." She could get used to having this guy around. He was eager to pitch in and looked good doing it. Since only a T-shirt and snug jeans covered those lovely muscles, she'd thoroughly enjoy some Dallas ogling.

After moving the screen and opening the flue, he picked up last week's edition of the *Sentinel*, tore off sheets of it and balled them up. "How do you see the big reveal playing out?"

"I'm not sure yet. I need to talk it over with Kendall. I was hoping the three of us could discuss it tomorrow, but Cheyenne wants to come by and check on us." Oh, yeah, watching Dallas crouched in front of her fireplace, his muscular back and arms on full display along with his tight buns, was a treat.

"I'm sure he'll hang around, probably want to help if he can. Is there any chance he suspects?"

"I didn't see any sign of it tonight, but one of my brothers will catch on soon. Before that happens, there's someone I need to tell."

"Who's that?" He struck a match and touched it to the newspaper under the grate.

"My mother."

"Desiree?" He popped up and turned to face her. "You're gonna tattle on your brothers?"

That made her grin. "I know it sounds like that, but—"

"It not only sounds like that, it *is* like that."

"Well, before you get all huffy about me being a tattletale, let me explain why this doesn't fit in that category."

"All right."

"Here's my definition of tattling. One of your siblings breaks the rules, and you run to Mom or Dad — in our case the Dad figure was our foreman Buck — and tell on them."

"And how is this different?"

"First of all, I didn't immediately run to my mom about it. Secondly, my brothers aren't breaking a family rule, they're butting into my business. Families do that all the time, including ours, but this crosses a line. And now that we're all adults, it's up to me to handle it, not my mother."

"Then why tell her?"

"To give her a heads up. I'm not asking her to do anything, but she might have some advice. She's at the center of the Rowdy Ranch universe and she deserves to know what's going on."

"Then why didn't your brothers tell her what they were up to?"

"Excellent question. My theory? They suspect she wouldn't like it. But they also might think they know best."

"I doubt she'd appreciate that attitude."

"That's putting it mildly."

<u>19</u>

Dallas left Angie to monitor the fire while he concentrated on making what he hoped would be a decent omelet they could split. A more thorough search of her cabinets yielded an unopened jar of sun-dried tomatoes. He'd use those instead of the salsa to give the omelet more bulk.

She had a decent array of spices although she must not use them much. Most jars were almost full. Once they could conduct this relationship out in the open, he'd cook her better meals than this. He'd find out her favorites and—

"Dallas, your phone's ringing!"

"Think I should answer?"

"Maybe. I'll bring it to you." She appeared a moment later with his phone. "It's stopped, but I saw the name and it's Clint."

"Fancy that." He slid a spatula around the edges of the omelet and folded it.

"That looks and smells delicious."

"Hope it will be." He turned down the heat and took the phone just as it pinged with a message. "Let's see what your brother's up to." He hit Play on the message.

Hey, Dallas, I'm working away on your cabinets and came up with a design change. I'd like to move forward with it tonight 'cause I'm on a roll, but first I need to show you what I'm talking about and make sure you're good with it. Could I pop over there for a few minutes? I promise it won't take long and then I can keep going.

Dallas sighed and glanced at Angie. "I think I have to let him come over, which means you need to eat your half while I'm gone."

"That's not right."

"Please. You're hungrier than I am. I had a late lunch with Beau after we picked up the tile. And this'll be so much better warm."

She looked torn.

"I want you to like my cooking and that means eating the food when it's at its best."

"Okay, if you insist."

"The potatoes are done and I've turned off the oven. We'll let the omelet cook a little more while I get dressed. I'll dish everything up before I leave. You can cover my plate with foil and stick it in the oven." He started out of the kitchen.

"You'll need to stall him off so you have time to get back home."

"Yes, ma'am. I'll wait and call him back once I'm out the door. I'll come up with some excuse for the delay." He made tracks for her bedroom.

He was mildly worried that the shit might prematurely hit the fan. Clint's call might be nothing more than excitement over the project. Cheyenne was probably just concerned about overworking his pregnant wife. But what if Angie's twin brothers were subconsciously tuning in to what was going on behind their backs?

When he walked back into the kitchen carrying his jacket, Angie stood by the stove gently nudging the omelet with the spatula. "I didn't want it to stick."

"It shouldn't. I kept the heat low enough and used lots of butter."

She glanced over her shoulder. "I brought your boots in. They're by the back door."

"Thank you. I'll go put 'em on and then come back and dish us up." He headed for the back door. "If you'd please take the potatoes out and grab some plates—"

"I'm on it." She laid the spatula on the spoon rest and went to get the plates. "I'm mad at Clint."

"He's excited about the cabinets." He tugged on his boots, put on his jacket and returned, using the spatula to transfer the omelet to one of the plates. "Which is a good thing. He's our only hope for matching the existing ones."

"I know." She put a hot pad on the counter and used potholders to bring over the baking dish. "But besides interfering in my business, he's interrupting our lovely dinner by the fire, a meal you produced out of practically no resources."

"He doesn't realize that." At least he hoped not.

She exhaled. "And you'll end up with excellent cabinets, which is great. I want you to have excellent cabinets."

"Thanks." He slid an arm around her waist and gave her a quick kiss. "I'm sure I'll love them."

After dividing the omelet in two, he spooned half the potatoes on one plate and the rest on the other.

"I can take it from here." She snatched a roll of foil out of a drawer. "The sooner you leave the sooner you'll be back."

"I'm outta here. Enjoy." Giving her another brief kiss, he took off, grabbing his hat and checking that his phone was in his pocket.

"I'll miss you!"

"I'll miss you, too!" He stepped outside and closed the door behind him. Brrr. Colder than when he'd made the trek over. Good thing he'd grabbed his hat. He pulled out his phone and called Clint, giving the excuse that he'd been attempting to wash dishes in the bathroom sink and hadn't heard the phone.

"I need ten minutes to clean up the bathroom. I made a mess. First time. I'll get better at it."

"Sure thing, buddy. I'll be over in ten."

"I'll be there." Whoops. "I mean, here." Disconnecting, he set off at a rapid clip. He hadn't timed himself on the way to Angie's, but he should have a chance to ditch his jacket before answering the door.

His story had some holes. If he'd been washing up dinner dishes, the house should smell like cooked food. Would Clint notice? If so, he'd say he had a sandwich.

The night was chilly enough for a fire, but that wouldn't be crackling away, either. He'd spent plenty of time raving about how much he loved that fireplace and stoked it up whenever possible.

Should he mention that he was too tired and planned to go to bed early?

Yeah, right. The mighty firefighter had worn himself out with a brief horseback ride and a road trip to Missoula and back. That excuse wouldn't work. He'd just hope Clint didn't ask too many questions.

An owl hooted in a nearby pine. Normally he'd stop and try to locate it. The moon was almost full and he could probably pinpoint its location. He'd been happy living in the sleepy little town of Wagon Train, but moving out here and seeing wildlife every single day had increased his happiness about a thousand percent.

When he was almost to his back door, the rumble of Clint's truck inspired him to jog the rest of the way. He took off his jacket on the way up the steps and hurried into his cabin. His very dark cabin. Yikes.

Hooking his jacket on a peg by the door, he ran through the place flipping switches. With luck, Clint hadn't noticed the lack of a friendly glow from the windows. But now he was panting. Not good. Clint likely wouldn't buy the idea that cleaning water off the bathroom floor had left him winded.

He'd mostly caught his breath when Clint rapped on the door. Taking one last gulp of air, he went to the door and opened it.

Clint looked at him and blinked. "Going somewhere?"

"No, why?"

"You're wearing your hat. I know you love that thing but—"

"Oh." He chuckled and hooked it on the rack by the door. "Forgot to take it off. I used a bucket to clean up the bathroom and I emptied it out back. Put on my hat out of habit."

Clint smiled. "I know how it is. I grab mine out of habit, too." He held up a legal pad. "I sketched out what I have in mind. So if we can have a sit-down so I can show you what—"

"Right, right!" He stepped back. "C'mon in. Can I offer you a beer?"

"No, thanks. That'll just make me sleepy and I want to work for another hour or so on this, assuming you like the plan."

"I'm sure I will." He gestured toward the sofa. "Have a seat."

"Surprised you don't have a fire going. We do, although Tyra's enjoying it by herself tonight. After dinner I went out to my shop to take some measurements and make sure this idea would work. It will."

Dallas ignored the comment about the fire and sat next to him. "Whatcha got?"

"The original cabinets on that side had a drawer under the counter and then doors under that with shelving behind the doors."

"And you were planning to make them roll-out shelves."

"I was, but then I saw this idea." He turned the legal pad in Dallas's direction, took a pen from his pocket and pointed to his sketches. "If you create two deep drawers, instead of doors and roll-out shelves, you have the same accessibility and it's one motion instead of two."

"I like it. Makes a lot of sense."

"Great. I was hoping you'd say that. I like it so much I'm thinking of reconfiguring our cabinets like that instead of the roll-out shelves I was planning on."

"You're putting in a lot of time on this."

"It's fun for me. And you're the kind of person who will appreciate the result. I wouldn't go to this much trouble for just anybody. You've become like family around here."

"I'm grateful for that, too. You've all been very good to me." Guilt pricked him a little, but it didn't stab him. Clint's motives weren't exactly pure.

That said, when the truth came out, Clint might not be so pleased that he'd knocked himself out making the cabinets.

Choosing to side with Angie had put him in the crosshairs. He accepted that. She was worth it.

_20_

Because she'd promised Dallas, Angie took several bites of the omelet and the potatoes. Sure enough, both tasted delicious. How had she missed that he could cook? That was like the prize in the cereal box.

She ate standing at the counter, and when she'd had enough to honestly say she'd enjoyed the food at its peak, she wrapped her plate in foil and stuck it next to his in the oven.

The first time he'd shown up at her back door she'd been taken by surprise. Not this time, and she'd rather set the scene than eat. After putting both pans to soak, she went back to the living room and added another log to the fire.

She'd started this adventure in her silky top and shorts, so why not put those back on? The sweats and sweatshirt had worked to fool Cheyenne, but she could ditch them now.

The bed could use some straightening, so she did that and turned back the covers. The bedside lamp she'd originally turned on was the only one lighting the room...and the remaining condoms lying on the table. The sight of those brought on a major tingle.

Switching on the lamp on the other side, she used the dimmer switch to lower the wattage on both. Instant atmosphere.

She'd installed dimmer switches throughout the house in anticipation of one day entertaining a man, preferably a cowboy, who had the potential to be a forever guy. That day — or rather night — had come.

Clad in her white silk, she returned to the living room and dimmed the lights on the chandelier. The lamps on either side of the couch were redundant with the light from the fire so she switched them off.

Now for the finishing touch. She opened a carved wooden chest tucked in a corner and pulled out the silver candlesticks she'd bought several months ago in preparation for the first ever romantic dinner for two on her beloved dining table.

She'd bought two white tapers the first part of this year, before her birthday. White signified new beginnings and matched her sexy nightwear. Back in February, when she and Dallas had picked up Smoky, her life had been going in exactly the direction she'd dreamed of.

Her brothers had derailed her, but she was back on track. She positioned two of her indigo placemats and cloth napkins on opposite sides of the dining table next to the window so she and Dallas could both see the fire. Indigo stood for opening new doors.

After closing all the curtains to keep out the chill and add a cozy factor, she added one more log to the fire. The substantial blaze shouldn't need tending for a while and the added heat meant she wouldn't shiver in her skimpy outfit.

She brought the box of matches over to the table so they'd be handy once Dallas arrived. No point in lighting the candles until she saw the whites of his eyes.

What else? Drinks and silverware. She'd recapped the beers and put them back in the fridge. Fetching two crystal goblets that had cost way too much but flashed rainbow colors in the light, she put them on the table. Champagne would have been nice, but beer would have to do.

She added silverware and eyed the table with satisfaction. Once the candles were lit it would look exactly the way she'd pictured a dinner here with the man of her choice. She hadn't cooked the meal, but that had always been a hazy part of the program.

A quick tap on the back door sent her running to open it. "That was fast."

"I jogged." He barreled in, breathing hard, nudged the door closed and drew her close. "God, you feel good."

"So do you." She wound her arms around his neck and settled in. "Cold, but good."

"Ah, geez. Let me get out of this jacket." Backing away, he yanked it off and hung it by the door. "And my boots." He toed them off. "And my doggone *hat.* I almost blew it when Clint arrived. I answered the door still wearing it." He left his hat on a peg and wrapped her in his arms. "Better?"

"I didn't mind your cold jacket. I'm just happy you're back. Did Clint make a comment about your hat?"

"He did, and I— never mind. It's all good. I don't think he suspects a thing." He glanced around the kitchen. "Was it this dark in here before?"

"I dimmed the lights."

He smiled. "And changed into my favorite outfit." He cupped her bottom and tucked her in closer. "Trying to drive me crazy?"

"Yes."

"At this rate my meal will get stone cold."

"No, it won't. We're going to have a nice dinner in front of the fire. We just need to get our plates out of the—"

"*Our* plates? You didn't eat yours?"

"I had several bites right after you left. So yummy. Then I covered my plate and stuck it in with yours so we could eat together."

His gaze softened. "That's very sweet."

"It's our first meal with just the two of us. It should be special."

"It will be." He hugged her tight and let her go. "Let's grab those plates."

She opened the oven, which was slightly warm but certainly not hot. "Should we heat things up?"

He laughed. "Done."

"I meant—"

"I know. Let's just eat it the way it is."

"Then here." She picked up both plates and handed them to him. "You take these and I'll bring our beer. I recapped those, too."

"Now I'm really glad I jogged back." He turned and started into the living room. "I didn't realize you'd— oh, hey. You weren't kidding about a special dinner. This is beautiful."

"I'm glad you like it." She pulled out the beer, a couple of coasters from a drawer and followed him.

"I love it. Does it matter where I sit?"

"You can choose. Just realize that people tend to stick with the same chair, so make sure you like whichever one you take."

"Then I'll take the one facing the front door." He put their plates on the table and removed the foil. "Okay if I light the candles?"

"Sure. You're the expert on fire, after all."

"Because I love it." He struck a match and touched the flame to each wick.

"You do?" She uncapped the bottles and filled both goblets. They were slender and didn't hold much, so she left the bottles on the coasters she'd brought. "I thought firefighters were all about, well, fighting fires."

"Well, sure, if it's threatening lives and destroying property." He blew out the match. "But fire itself fascinates me. It's powerful, beautiful and dangerous. Without the discovery of fire, it would be—"

"Dark. Very dark."

He laughed. "Well said."

"Then you don't frown at the use of candles?"

"Not at all. I'm glad you got them out. Since this is such a romantic setting, will you let me pull out your chair?"

"Sure." The seat was a wee bit cold on her tush.

"It's really an excuse to do this." Leaning down, he swept her hair aside and kissed the curve of her neck, his breath warm on her skin.

"Mm." The velvet touch of his lips heated up her tush along with every cell in her body. "That's nice."

"There's more where that came from." He rounded the table and took his seat across from her.

"I sure hope so."

"I'm ready and willing, but we keep getting interrupted."

"I've noticed." She lifted her goblet. "To several undisturbed hours together."

"I'll drink to—" He tilted his head in the direction of the kitchen. "Unless you set a timer...."

"It's my phone." She sighed and put down her glass. "That's my mom's ring. I'd better get it."

"Go ahead. I'll put the foil back on."

"Good idea. Be right back." Hurrying into the kitchen, she snatched her phone from the counter. "Hey, Mom, what's up?"

"I don't know exactly, but something is."

"Like what?" She was prepared to tell her the whole story, but not when Dallas was waiting in the next room.

"I can't put my finger on it, but there's something weird about how your brothers are reacting to this flooding incident. Or I should say, overreacting."

"In what way?" The phone call wasn't a surprise. Not much got past her mom.

"They're hovering."

She swallowed a laugh. Perfect word. "Now that you mention it, I suppose they are."

"For example, Tyra was here a little while ago. She came over to borrow a book because Clint's out in his shop burning the midnight oil working on the cabinets. She's not complaining, because he's doing a good deed, but—"

"They're newlyweds and they both have the night off. I get it." And so would her mother once she knew the score.

"Then this afternoon I called Jess about something I plan to buy Maverick for her birthday, and she mentioned Beau was in Missoula sourcing tile."

"Yep, he's really into this project, too."

"Which is nice of him, but he usually spends Saturday afternoons with Mav. Oh, and yesterday Gil accidentally sent me a text meant for Cheyenne. I'll read it to you. *Hey, bro, Dallas wants a horseshoe door knocker. Mentioned it weeks ago. I just remembered and unearthed one. Tomorrow would be a good time for me to deliver it, if you know what I mean. Any objections?*

"Did he realize he'd texted you?" She walked to the door of the kitchen, blew Dallas a kiss and got a sexy smile in return.

"Right away. He sent another one apologizing. I thought about asking why he'd said *if you know what I mean* but then I shrugged it off. Now I'm putting it together with the cabinet frenzy and the rush to pick up tile, and I'm wondering if there's more than good Samaritan instincts in play."

"Sounds like you're onto something." She strolled toward the dining table. "Kendall and I are only working a half-day tomorrow. Any chance we can come over for a late lunch, say around one-thirty, so we can talk about this?"

"By all means. I'd like to get her opinion. Cheyenne seems really on edge, too, and I don't think it's just the leak bugging him. How about if we include Marybeth?"

"Perfect. See you then. Bye, Mom." She disconnected and gazed at Dallas. "She thinks her boys are acting strange."

"Are you going to tell her about us?"

"I'd like to. Are you okay with it?"

His gaze warmed. "Are you kidding? I'm ready to tell the world."

Ahhh. The guy sure did know his lines.

21

Dallas didn't mind a bit that Desiree would soon learn about this relationship. She liked him and loved Angie. Unlike her sons, she'd be happy for them. But telling her likely would have consequences. That made tonight even more precious.

Angie returned to her seat and picked up her goblet. "As I was saying...."

He lifted his glass and touched it to hers. "To tonight. Thank you for inviting me."

"To tonight..." She met his gaze. "And many more like it."

Promising. "Minus the interruptions."

She grinned. "Amen to that." She sipped her beer. "I'm pretending it's champagne."

"If I'd had some in the fridge I would have brought it." He took a hefty swallow. "If I'm the first guy who's been in your bedroom, I'm guessing you don't use these candlesticks much, either."

"Nope." Putting down her goblet, she picked up her fork. "This is their first outing."

"They look great." He started eating, too. Lukewarm food wasn't his preference, but at least it tasted decent. "When did you buy them?"

"At a Christmas clearance sale in January. Ditto the candles. The placemats and napkins I found last summer."

"You've probably used them before, though."

"Actually, I haven't. Whenever it's just me, or I have someone over, I have straw ones that you can wipe clean."

"Then I'll be careful."

"Don't worry about it. They wash."

"I'll still be careful. And I have another toast." He raised his goblet.

"Go for it." Smiling, she lifted hers.

"To you, for trusting that I won't mess this up. And I'm not talking about the placemats."

"You won't." She tapped her glass to his and took a drink.

He followed suit and set it down so he could dig into his meal. "How can you be so sure?"

"I've been watching you." She spread two fingers, pointed to her eyes and then his before she went back to eating.

That cracked him up. "I don't believe that. You ignored me completely until your birthday party."

"That shows how much you know. I have unique skills I developed as the youngest in a big family loaded with boys. Stealthy observation is my superpower."

He looked across the table. "You're adorable."

"I know, and I use that to my advantage, too."

She certainly did, and he longed to sweep her up and carry her adorable self to the bedroom. He was heating up just like the logs crackling and popping in the fireplace. But until it died down, they couldn't leave it unattended.

Besides, she'd anticipated a romantic dinner for quite a while. No reason to rush it. "I wish I had your confidence in me. This is a tricky maneuver we're attempting."

"But you took it on without hesitation. That shows courage."

"Easy choice. Once I knew how much you wanted me, game over."

"I like that in a person." She popped the last bit of food into her mouth.

"Too bad your brothers don't feel the same."

She chewed and swallowed. "I'm determined that they'll see the light eventually. That's why I need to talk to Mom tomorrow. And Marybeth, who's like a mom. She's been there ever since I was born. I don't want to screw this up, either. I realize how much you're risking."

"Just so you know, so do I, and I don't regret throwing in with you. No second thoughts."

"I promise I won't let my brothers make you the bad guy."

"Don't worry. If it comes to that, I'll handle it. Just so you consider me the good guy."

"Always." She glanced at his almost empty plate. "I overestimated how long it would take us to eat. I built up the fire so we wouldn't have to tend it during dinner, but now we can't safely leave it."

He smiled. "We can linger over our beer."

"Are you in a lingering mood? Because I'm not."

Pushing back his chair, he stood and blew out the candles. "Let's go make out on your couch."

"Awesome idea." She slipped out of her chair. "I've never made out on that couch."

He met her halfway and put his arm around her waist as they started toward the couch. "I'm ridiculously happy about that."

"Seems you kinda like being the first romantic encounter I've had in this cabin."

"I do. I was a little overwhelmed in the beginning, but now I'm into it." He plopped down on the couch, bringing her down with him.

"Me, too." And just like that, she straddled his thighs, cupped his face and moved in for a kiss that left him gasping.

Lifting her mouth slightly and keeping her grip on his jaw, she gulped for air. "Sorry if I'm blocking your view of the fire."

"I didn't come over here to stare at it." Cradling the back of her head, he pulled her back into the kiss, thrusting his tongue into her hot, sweet mouth.

She got busy unbuttoning his shirt. He didn't have to unbutton anything. Her satin tank top offered no resistance as he pulled it up and over her breasts. Leaning back, she caught the hem in both hands, tugged it over her head and tossed it on the floor.

With her silky breasts filling his hands and her tongue in his mouth he was on sensory overload. The heat from the blaze only feet away mimicked the fire racing through his veins. As the party ramped up below his belt, a familiar ache reminded him he'd left all the condoms on her nightstand.

Meanwhile she'd opened his shirt and started working on his jeans. She had the buckle unfastened and the metal button undone when she lifted her head. "We need an item from the bedroom."

He dragged in a breath. "Yes, ma'am."

"I'll get it." She hopped off his lap.

He opened his eyes in time to catch her dashing toward the hall wearing only the tiny satin shorts. He kept his eyes open so he wouldn't miss her topless reentry. And it was a showstopper.

She returned as quickly as she'd left, her cheeks flushed, her hair reflecting the light from the fire and her breasts quivering with each quick step. He couldn't have wiped the smile off his face if someone had offered him a million bucks.

She laughed. "You haven't moved an inch."

"Some of me has."

"I thought maybe you'd have your jeans off by now."

"And risk missing the dazzling entrance you just made?" He got to his feet and unzipped his fly.

"A boobs man, are you?" She gave him a shimmy.

He worked faster. "No favorites. I like it all, hint, hint."

"Me, too, hint, hint. Catch." She tossed him a condom.

He made a miraculous catch considering she followed the toss by wiggling out of her satin shorts and kicking them away.

"Hey, statue man, it's just me. You've seen it all before."

"Not like this." He sucked in air. "Not when you're bathed in firelight. Do you even know how beautiful you are?"

She swallowed. "You could turn a girl's head with speeches like that."

"I sure hope so. Of all the heads in the world, yours is the one I most want to turn."

She started toward him, a gleam of arousal in her blue eyes. "Keep talking this way and you'll get what you want." Her voice grew husky. "As often as you want it."

Lust fried his brain. "Um..."

"Cat got your tongue?" She came just close enough for her nipples to graze his chest. "Let's get rid of that shirt." She peeled it off his shoulders and kept pulling until the cuffs cleared his hands. Then she dropped it. "Now for the rest."

He could take off his own jeans. Been doing it for years. But having her undress him while they stood in the middle of her living room was surprisingly erotic.

Especially the way she did it, her breasts nudging his chest, his abs, his cock as she shoved his jeans and briefs to the floor. Yep, intentional nudging. And he was a churning mass of testosterone neediness.

After he stepped free, she plucked the condom packet from his unresisting fingers, opened it and rolled on the condom with brisk efficiency.

Holding his gaze, she placed her palms on his chest. "Move back."

One step and his calves brushed the fabric of the couch. He sat on the still-warm cushion. The suede texture had a lot more sensual impact on his bare butt than when he'd touched it with his hand.

Then she joined him, adding the silken pressure of her thighs resting on his. The twinge of an impending orgasm made his breath hitch.

"You okay?"

"Never better."

Taking hold of his shoulders, she rose to her knees. "Want to guide me in?"

"Oh, yeah." Adrenaline shot through him as he grasped her firm behind. The lady was exceedingly touchable. Centering her over his eager cock, he brought her down slowly, heart pounding, until he was buried to the hilt in her warmth.

He closed his eyes, savoring the moment. In the past, he'd questioned the possibility of a perfect mate, doubted that two people could fit together like pieces of a puzzle. Doubts gone. Question answered.

She moaned softly and dug her fingers into his shoulders. "I don't want to come yet."

"Me, either."

Releasing her grip, she shoved her hands through his hair and kissed him again, slackening her jaw, going deep. He wrapped her in his arms and held her tight, beating heart to beating heart.

He never wanted to let go.

22

Sex had never been so wonderful. Angie couldn't get close enough to Dallas, couldn't stop kissing him. She would happily stay in the snug circle of his arms, intimately linked, forever.

Or maybe not. His cock twitched. She gave him an involuntary squeeze. He groaned and rocked his hips, creating delicious friction, striking the match. And she was on fire, her hips pumping as he urged her on.

She didn't last long. Crying out as her climax arrived, she gripped his broad shoulders and abandoned herself to the glorious ride. Wave after wave rolled through her trembling body. "Come with me!"

"Not yet." His breath hissed out between clenched teeth. Then he surrendered with a roar. Head thrown back, he shuddered beneath her.

Panting, she rested her forehead on his shoulder, her hand braced against his sweaty chest. "Your heart's going really fast."

"No kidding." He gulped. "That was epic."

She looked up. "Did the couch pass the test?"

He lifted his head and met her gaze. His slow smile turned into a chuckle. "You say the damnedest things."

"So I've been told." She grinned. "Should I keep the couch or not?"

"We should have it bronzed."

"Now who's being silly?"

"Me." He cupped her face. "Silly, crazy, having a blast getting to know you." He gave her a gentle kiss and drew back. "But now I have to ask you to climb off so I can take care of business."

"Then what?"

His dark eyes flashed with amusement. "We'll do the dishes and go to bed, of course."

"I have a dishwasher."

"And two pans that need scrubbing."

"That can wait. I'll clear the table while you're taking care of the condom situation. I'll meet you in bed."

"Unless I meet you in the kitchen first. Ever tried naked dish washing?"

"You have?"

"No. Could be fun, though. Another first time experience."

"Okay, you win. Come find me in the kitchen." She moved carefully as she disengaged.

"I'll see if I can spot you."

She laughed as she headed back to the table to grab their plates and empty goblets. "You can't miss me. I'll be the naked lady pulling all the curtains closed."

Which she did, quickly. Neither of the windows could be seen from the road. Probably.

She'd never had to worry about it, so she wasn't sure.

After dumping the water she'd left in each of the pans, she set them beside the sink, put the stopper in the drain and turned on the hot water. He had a point about the pans. And she'd planned to hand-wash the goblets so she might clean the plates, too.

She squirted dish soap into the sink and laid a goblet into the warm, sudsy water.

"A sight like that could permanently destroy the dishwasher industry."

She glanced over her shoulder.

Dallas leaned in the doorway, his muscular body on full display as he sipped from one of the beer bottles she'd left on the table. He held out the other one. "Care to join me?"

Strolling toward him, she gave him an appreciative once-over. "Are we drinking beer or washing dishes?"

"Both." Pushing away from the door frame, he surveyed her, his gaze making her tingle all over. "Gotta stay hydrated when you're working hard." He handed over the bottle.

"Thanks for watching out for me." Closing her eyes, she took a long, slow pull on the bottle.

"Oh, I'm watching, all right."

She opened her eyes and grinned. "I was counting on it. Did I get a rise out of you?" Her gaze dropped. "Oh, look. I did."

"You sure are saucy for a lady who's never participated in naked dish washing. Are you sandbagging me?"

"Nope." She turned around and put a sway in her walk as she went back to the sink. "Just a fast learner." Snatching a cotton dishtowel from a hook by the sink, she tossed it in his direction. "I'm washing. You can dry."

"Nice towel. Soft."

"I like them." She plunged her hands into the sudsy water, located the dishcloth she'd dropped in earlier and began carefully washing the delicate goblet. "I have to admit this is a turn-on."

He stepped up behind her. "I want to help wash."

"Oh, like I didn't see that coming." She glanced over her shoulder. "But it's really a one-person job."

"Not if one person is blindfolded." He folded the dishtowel and held it up, eyebrows raised.

Her pulse raced. "Doesn't sound very efficient."

"Could be fun. If you can't see, you'll be more into how that warm water feels."

"You're the sandbagger. I'll bet you've done—"

"Never. Just making it up as I go along. You inspire me."

"Ditto." She reveled in the heat of his gaze. "Okay, why not?"

"Hold still." He laid the folded towel across her eyes and tied it behind her head. "Can you see?"

"I can't."

"Then here we go." He slid his hands into the fragrant, soapy water and wove his fingers through hers.

Her breathing quickened. His solid presence behind her, some of him growing more solid by the second, was exciting. She tightened her grip on the goblet.

"Careful with the glass. Looks like it could break real easy."

Whoops. She relaxed her fingers. "You should probably let go of my hands."

"I will if you can't do it, but just try. I like this. Reminds me of an old Patrick Swayze movie."

"*Ghost.* You watched it?"

"Uh-huh." He leaned down and kissed her bare shoulder. "Sexy."

"Mm." She shivered in anticipation. Dallas had more facets than the Hope diamond. Living with him would be one adventure after anoth— *whoa, girl. Don't be getting ahead of yourself.*

She focused on the challenge of washing the goblet without snapping the stem. "Time to rinse it."

"I'll do that." He let go of her hands and water rushed from the faucet into the opposite sink. "Done. Want a sip of your beer?"

"Sure." She lifted one hand out of the water.

He guided it back into the water. "Let me."

The bottle touched her lips. Would it end up all over her? Nope. He tilted it just enough to give her a sip, then took it away.

"Where did you learn that?"

"Nursing my little brother one winter when he got sick."

Another clue to the makeup of Dallas Armstrong. "He's okay, though, right?"

"Oh, yeah. Healthy as a horse. Here's the next glass."

They repeated the routine and she got better at it. The plates were a breeze, but the pans took more effort. He stopped several times to deliver sips of beer. Then he started adding kisses to the beer breaks.

"Let's leave the pans." The huskiness in his voice betrayed that his mind was drifting elsewhere. The brush of his cock whenever he shifted his weight was the clincher.

When he cupped her breasts in his warm, sudsy hands, she laughed and pulled off the blindfold. "I think we're done, here."

He stroked his thumbs over her nipples. "How could you tell?"

"Lucky guess." His warm, damp caress was all she needed to tip her over into a full-blown case of lust. The sensual dishwater game had primed her for exactly what he had in mind.

Sliding his grip to her shoulders, he turned her to face him. "I love touching you."

She basked in the glow of his gaze. "I love it when you do."

"Thank you for indulging me."

"I pretended you were Patrick Swayze."

"Well, damn it."

"No, I didn't." She wound her wet arms around his neck. "You're the only guy in my head."

"And your bed, hint, hint?"

"Right after I dry that crystal. If I don't it'll have water spots."

"Let me." He took the dishtowel.

"Then I'll go warm up the bed." She left the kitchen, and her precious goblets, in his hands. They were safe there. So was she.

23

Dallas polished the glasses the way he figured Angie would have done it. Her trust in him was humbling. But not misplaced. If she wanted a champion, he was her guy, even if it meant standing up to her brothers, including his best friend.

When he was satisfied that the glasses had zero water spots, he set them carefully on the counter and hung up the towel. Better grab his phone and set the alarm.

The hours were slipping by faster than he'd like. He could easily lose track of time and forget he had to be gone before sunup.

After pulling the phone out of his jacket pocket, he set the alarm. Then he took it with him as he left the kitchen, turning off the lights on his way out.

The fire had been reduced to a few glowing embers. Removing the screen, he shoveled some ash over those that were still winking at him and replaced the screen.

Where were his clothes? Last time he'd been in this spot they'd been strewn all over the place. Her silk outfit, too. She must have picked them up.

He gave the room a quick glance before locating the dimmer switch that controlled the chandelier. Great touch. He might find out how much Bret and Gil would charge him for one. Assuming he wasn't on their permanent shit list after he and Angie went public.

He really liked that chandelier, though. Liked the whole place. Did he love it the way he loved his? That was a tough one. He'd hate to have to make a choice.

Angie greeted him propped up in bed, the covers pulled up to her waist. She flashed him a grin. "I was ready to send out a search party. You must have done a heck of a job on those goblets."

He held up his phone. "I took time to grab this and set my alarm."

"Oh, good thought."

"And I banked the fire." He started toward his side of the bed. He recognized it by the condom packets on the nightstand.

"Thank you. Speaking of fires, we have one in here, too."

"We do?" He paused to look around. Sure enough, flames danced inside an electric fireplace on the wall opposite the end of the bed. Nice one, too, with a mantel and a hearth. "Has that been here all along?"

"Sure has."

"Can't believe I missed it." He pulled back the covers and climbed into bed.

"You've been mesmerized by my beauty." She scooted down and rolled to face him.

"Yes, ma'am, that's a fact." He tugged her close. "Noticed all those books, though."

"That's why I wanted a fireplace in here, so I could have a fire while I read in bed."

"Good thing it's not wood-burning, then."

"That's what Mom thought. She could see me falling asleep with a book and waking up to find the place in flames. But I'd rather have the real thing."

"I understand." He nuzzled the side of her neck. "I love fire, too."

Tunneling her fingers through his hair, she arched into his caress. "I love the smell, the sound. No two fires are the same."

He lifted his head, craving the heat smoldering in her blue eyes, the invitation in her parted lips. "Just like making love."

"Just like that."

The husky note in her voice sent lightning through his veins. "Let's set this bed on fire."

With a soft moan, she pulled his head down, her kiss ravenous as she tangled her body with his. He rolled her to her back, pinning her to the mattress, drowning in a tsunami of need. *Angie.*

He almost forgot the condom. Almost. At the last minute, he forced himself to stop kissing her. "Condom." His voice rasped like a rusty gate.

"Hurry."

Stretching toward the nightstand, he snagged one and set a world record putting it on. As he plunged his cock into her slick channel, he let out a bellow that would make a bull moose proud. So good. *So good.*

Angie's breathless laugh was music to his ears. She gripped his butt and wound her legs around his while they rocked that bed so hard it squeaked.

Her jubilant cry of *I'm coming* put him to the test. Her gasps and the rhythmic clenching of her hot core challenged him, but he already had two climaxes under his belt.

He kept going, thrusting hard and fast. "Again, sweet lady. Come for me again."

And she did, shouting, cussing and crying out his name. That last part, hearing his name while she was out of her mind with pleasure, was the best of all. Time to bring it on home.

Slipping the reins on his control, he pushed deep and... oh... yeah, oh, yeah, *oh yeah*! The blast launched him on a rocket ride to outer space — couldn't see, couldn't hear, but damn could he *feel.* Never like this. Never. Like. This.

Gradually the roaring in his ears settled down. And he could breathe again. Sort of. Slowly he opened his eyes and looked down at Angie's smiling face.

She reached up and touched his cheek. "Have a good time?"

He opened his mouth. Nothing came out.

"I'll take that as a yes."

He nodded. It was the best he could do. His language skills had been fried by the best sex of his life.

* * *

Eventually Dallas gathered his forces enough to accomplish the condom chore. After washing up, he returned to cuddle with Angie. She had an uncommon number of pillows, which meant they could use them to lean on while they looked at the fire.

He wrapped his arm around her and she laid her head on his shoulder. He couldn't remember the last time he'd been this relaxed. "I like the fire just fine. It's pretty."

"I'll admit it looks better after two orgasms."

"The whole world looks better after a session like we just had."

"I know, right? I didn't realize how much I missed..." She trailed off.

He gave her a squeeze. "Now you have to tell me how long it's been."

"Only if you go first."

"Oh, that's easy. I had a little something going last spring, but after I moved out to the ranch, nothing."

"Why?"

"I caught sight of you and ended the other relationship."

Lifting her head off his shoulder, she stared at him. "Even when I didn't give you the time of day?"

He shrugged. "Time was on my side. You didn't seem to be with anybody. Sooner or later I would have created a one-on-one conversation and made my case. You beat me to it."

"Made your case?" She grinned. "What were you going to say?"

"The usual — I have all my teeth, twenty-twenty vision and I know how to properly clean a bathroom."

She cracked up. "That's an impressive resume."

"Just filling in the blanks. You could have been avoiding me because you assumed I was wearing dentures, contacts, and I'd never scrubbed a toilet in my life."

"Yeah, you nailed it. I'm so relieved to hear I was so wrong about you." She frowned. "Wait, you didn't take yourself totally off the market. You had a date with Tyra a few days before my party."

"True. How did you hear about it?"

"The way I hear about everything. From Kendall. She had no idea I had you in my sights. She was just passing on a tidbit of gossip."

"What did she say?"

"That you had her over for dinner, but according to Cheyenne, you two didn't click."

"We didn't. She wasn't interested in me and now we know why."

"Were you interested in her, though? You must have been if you—"

He sighed. "Cheyenne urged me to give it a shot. I didn't want to tell him the truth, that I was waiting for you. And the whole Valentine's Day thing was getting to me. I'd started wondering if I was being a stubborn idiot. Inviting Tyra over was a test."

"Not a very good one since she was in love with my brother. If she'd shown interest, would you have done anything about it?"

"Like what?"

"Like kiss her, make out, take her to—"

"Whoa, whoa, none of the above. The test worked because I was relieved that she wasn't into me. Could have been awkward otherwise."

"I would say so. You did invite her over, after all."

"And I shouldn't have. The whole time I sat there wishing you were sitting across from me instead."

"I accept the invitation."

He chuckled. "Tomorrow night?"

"You don't have a sink."

"All I need is a stove."

"Then I'm in."

"It's a deal, but don't think you've distracted me. I've told you my story. What's yours?"

"Coincidentally, I had something going last spring, too."

He clenched his jaw. He wasn't proud of that unevolved reaction. But thinking of her with someone else stirred primitive emotions. "And?"

"I saw you at the bachelor auction and broke up with that guy."

"You broke up with him because of me and then gave me the cold shoulder?"

"It must sound crazy, but—"

"It would if I hadn't seen your brothers at work once you did approach me."

"Exactly."

"You mentioned dating guys from out of town. Was he?"

"Yes."

He sighed with relief.

Which earned him a light punch on the shoulder. "What if he was from here? What then?"

"I'd look him up so I could convince myself he didn't deserve you. Not that *I* deserve you, but I'd want him to be less deserving than me."

"He is less deserving."

"Good."

"Does your ex live here?"

"Not anymore."

"Good." She held his gaze. "When we confront my brothers, we're telling them about this long-term infatuation. It was almost a year."

"Infatuation? Let's find a better word."

"How do you like crush?"

"I don't."

"Besotted?"

He grinned. "I like it. We were besotted with each other."

"Immersed in besottedness."

"And speaking of immersion, we have two condoms left."

"Then kiss me, you besotted fool. The night is young."

"My pleasure, sweet besotted lady." The night wasn't young, though. The minutes were racing by fast, too fast. When he reached for the condom he turned his phone face down.

24

In the dim light of approaching dawn, Angie kissed Dallas goodbye a million times and finally had to let him go. Watching him walk away was tough.

But spending the morning in his house pretending to hate his guts was worse. Beau was the fly in the ointment. Soon after she and Kendall had prepped the laundry room floor, he'd arrived and offered to operate the wet saw set up outside the cabin.

He'd learned how during the installation of his floor and had become good at cutting tile, of course. That was Beau for you. Excelled at everything.

Angie had already planned to be the tile cutter on this job. Kendall normally handled it, but the horrendous screeching at close range wouldn't be good for the baby. It wasn't like they could give little snookums ear plugs.

The work wouldn't proceed as fast — Kendall was a better cutter and Angie was a faster tiler. She hadn't bothered to explain that to Beau when he'd raved to Dallas about their incredible speed.

Evidently he'd had time to figure it out, and was here to get 'er done. She'd warned him he wasn't getting paid, and he'd shrugged that off with a joke. Then he'd invited Dallas to come outside and be his assistant, neatly separating her from the man of her dreams.

Oh, she got to see Dallas. He was the go-between, taking marked tile out to Beau and bringing back the cut ones. Her brother must be in rare form. Those two were yukking it up, their laughter filtering in whenever the saw wasn't going.

Meanwhile she was stuck with brief, meaningful glances and the occasional brush of his hand. Torture.

"I thought Cheyenne would be the one crashing our tiling party," she muttered as Dallas went back outside.

"I gave him a list of chores as long as a horse's leg." Kendall pressed tile into the layer of thinset and added spacers. They were taking turns since the laundry room was too small for them to work together. "I promised him a batch of sugar cookies if they were all done when I got home this afternoon."

Angie took a swig from her water bottle and eyed their progress. With Beau on the job, they'd be done in no time. "Too bad Jess didn't have a list like that for my brother."

"For all we know she did, but he's convinced her this is a priority."

"Do you think he's told her why he's so gung-ho to get it done?"

Kendall shook her head. "Jess would have hit the roof."

"I think so, too. Same with Tyra if she knew why Clint was busting his butt constructing those cabinets."

"I can't wait to hear your mom on the subject."

"Speaking of that, I'm going to text her and see if we can come over early. We'll be done way before one-thirty." She located her phone sitting on the kitchen counter. It was covered with stacked pots and pans from the ruined cabinets.

"Good. I'm starving."

Angie checked the paper bag Kendall had brought. "Looks like you finished off the cheese and crackers. Want me to ask Dallas if we can raid his fridge?"

"Nah. If we'll be finished soon I'll wait for lunch. It'll taste that much better if I'm hungry."

"Okay, then." A quick text to her mom received an instant reply — *come over whenever you're finished.* "You're in luck, Ken. Mom says we can come whenever."

"Great."

"And it's time for you to take a break."

"You don't have to tell me twice." She stood and stretched her lower back before she walked into the kitchen. "It's all yours."

"Are you okay? Promise you'll tell me if you get—"

"I'm fine. Breaks are good though."

"We'll schedule plenty tomorrow. As many as you need." She took Kendall's place and spread thinset on the final section.

"Do you know if Beau's planning on coming over tomorrow, too?"

"He already said he would. He moved a couple of clients to later in the week to free up the time." She pressed down one tile, then another. Normally she loved this process. But frustration dogged her as she worked.

"I hate his ulterior motive for coming over here, but I think he's genuinely concerned about protecting the munchkin from high decibels."

"Of course he is. He's wonderful. And so misguided."

"At least with his help, we'll get the bulk of the tiling done tomorrow. Have you talked to the Emersons?"

"This morning before you picked me up." She'd been so busy filling Kendall in on last night's drama that she hadn't mentioned it. "I told them we'll be starting on the porch Tuesday afternoon instead of tomorrow, like we'd planned."

"They're okay with that?"

"They said it doesn't matter since they're leaving town. I figure we'll dovetail the two jobs for the rest of this week." *Dallas will be on duty. Out of reach.* "We'll still be able to finish the porch before they come home on Saturday."

"Sounds good. Hey, you're rocking that job, Ang. You're one fast tiler."

"Thanks." She sat back on her heels and wiped her forehead with her sleeve. "When Dallas brings back the ones I gave him, I'll set those and we're done with this part."

"Yay. I can taste Marybeth's potato salad already. I know she'll make it if she knows I'm coming over."

"I'm sure she will. Did Cheyenne ask if he could go?"

"I could tell he wanted to be invited. I told him we're getting together to discuss the subject of virginity."

"I'll bet that cooled his jets."

"Pretty much. But for good measure I added that your mom's thinking of writing a character who's a virgin and she wants to consult with someone who remembers what it's like. In detail."

She grinned. "Nicely played."

* * *

After the last tile was laid, Dallas offered his guest bathroom sink to Angie and Kendall so they could wash up before going to lunch. Meanwhile the guys would transfer the wet saw to the porch, cover it and tidy up the outside work area.

On the way to the bathroom, Angie glanced into Dallas's bedroom, the setting she'd intended for the launch of their secret affair. The room looked like him — a wool Pendleton blanket folded neatly at the foot of his bed, a Remington print on the wall, a rag rug on the floor, some framed family pictures on the dresser.

Kendall chuckled. "Think you'll end up there tonight?"

"We will if all goes as planned." She continued down the hall and motioned for Kendall to take the first turn at the sink. "Might depend on what Mom says at lunch."

"Do you think she'll want to call a family meeting for tonight?"

A chill ran through her. "I guess that's a possibility. And although I want this settled, I...."

"Want one more night with Dallas before the poo-poo hits the propeller?" Kendall reached for a towel and stepped aside to give Angie access to the sink.

"You guessed it." She turned on the water and soaped up. I—"

"Cool it." Kendall lowered her voice. "They just came back in. Keep chatting or they'll think we're up to something."

Which we are. "Yeah, I agree about the Emerson job. Sure hope the weather holds. I'm looking forward to working outside."

"Me, too. I think working outside is my favorite."

"Our first screened-in porch." She took the towel Kendall handed her.

"Should be interesting. And if I like the way it turns out, I can see a project coming up for Cheyenne and me. A screened porch would be a great place to sit with the baby."

"Absolutely. If you decide to do that, let me—" She swallowed the rest of her comment when Dallas appeared in her peripheral vision, headed their way.

He paused just outside the door. "Beau invited me to his place for lunch. Everything's been put away, and we used the hose to get the worst of it off us. We'll be leaving shortly."

She nodded, tongue-tied just looking at his gorgeous self, sleeves rolled back, dark hair tousled, shirt damp from where he'd splashed himself with the hose. Or more likely, Beau had splashed him.

The cotton clung lovingly to his broad chest. Yum. A smudge of something decorated his cheek. She fisted both hands to keep from wiping it off.

He paused, his dark gaze holding hers. "Enjoy your lunch with your mom."

"Thanks."

He walked away, giving her a swoon-worthy view of his broad shoulders and tight buns. She stood still, following his loose-hipped stride until he was out the door.

"You've got it bad."

"I know."

"Here's the good news. He does, too."

She swallowed. "Yeah, that is good news."

"C'mon, girlfriend." Kendall gave her arm a squeeze. "Let's go tie on the feedbag at your mom's house."

"Let's do." She glanced at his bedroom once more as they passed by. "Just like a firefighter. So neat."

"That's another reason you two are meant for each other. You like things tidy. I'm not crazy that Cheyenne has to be gone several nights a week and yeah, it's a dangerous job, but his training in keeping things shipshape is lovely."

"I look forward to the day I can enjoy all his wonderful traits."

"I predict it'll come sooner than you think. Talking with your mom's a good next step. Moving on."

"In a minute." She gave her precious friend a bear hug. "Thank you for being there."

"Always."

Kendall's dazzling smile warmed her heart. No wonder Cheyenne called her Sunshine.

25

When Dallas and Beau arrived, Jess met them at the door, car keys in hand. "Sandwich fixings are in the fridge and I just put Mav down for a nap. You guys are in charge."

Beau's eyebrows rose. "You going somewhere?"

"Just over to your mom's for lunch."

"Why?"

"We need to coordinate plans for Mav's birthday party."

"Three months away?"

"And it'll be here before you know it. Bye." She stepped around them and whisked out the door.

Beau shook his head. "I love my daughter dearly, but don't you think *coordinating*—" He paused to make air quotes. "Her first birthday party three months out is a wee bit extreme?"

"She is your mom's first grandchild." He kept his expression neutral. At least he hoped he did. He could be jumping to conclusions, but it looked to him like Desiree was rallying the troops. He'd love to know if Tyra had been invited to this gathering.

"I get that it's her first grandchild. And Maverick's a girl on top of it, but a big production makes no sense to me and I doubt she'll appreciate it, either. She isn't old enough for all the bells and whistles."

"Are you going to object?"

He paused, took off his hat, scratched his head and repositioned the hat. "Don't reckon I am. Let me go look in on Mav. Then we'll build us some sandwiches."

"Great." As Beau walked down the hall toward Maverick's room, Dallas felt something rubbing against his leg. He glanced down. Bright green eyes blinked at him.

Crouching, he scratched behind the black cat's ears, resulting in a loud purr. Made him smile. He'd grown up with cats and dogs in the house. Missed that, but a firefighter's life didn't lend itself to having a pet.

"I see Midnight's found himself a new friend."

Dallas looked up. "I didn't know you had a cat."

"He was likely conked out when you were here yesterday. Midnight's the one who forced me to conquer my demons. I owe that cat big time."

"Sounds like a story."

"A short one. Midnight's Jess's cat. First night Jess and I got cozy, I accidentally used a condom Midnight had chewed on. Didn't notice in the heat of the moment, if you take my meaning."

"I do." He'd had several of those moments recently. "That's when Jess got pregnant?"

"Bingo."

Dallas snorted, then regretted it. "Sorry. I shouldn't laugh, but—"

"Sure you should. It's hilarious."

"I'll bet it wasn't at the time, though."

"No, sir. But now I thank him every morning when I feed him his breakfast. He's my hero."

"Probably your mom's, too."

"Oh, yeah, she brings him a treat every time she comes over. Hey, you hungry?"

"I could eat." He gave Midnight one last scratch and stood.

"Let's build us some sandwiches and take 'em out on the back porch. That way we can watch those pigs and they can watch us. They like seeing me sittin' on the porch."

"Works for me." He took a deep breath and followed Beau into the kitchen. Angie's brother was a hard guy to be angry with. If only he could level with Beau and discuss the problem man-to-man. But he'd promised Angie he wouldn't take any action.

Moments later, he took the Adirondack chair closest to the side railing and Beau claimed the one near the steps. They set their beers on the small table between them.

Beau settled his plate in his lap and picked up his beer. "See that? They're gettin' up, hurrying over to the fence, making noise and waggin' their tails. Hey, Slim! Hey, Pickens!"

Dallas grinned. Sure enough, the pigs were talking to Beau, making gruff little *huh-huh-huh* sounds. Pickens, the black and white one talked louder than his bigger, all-black brother, but they were both chatty.

"I brought 'em some treats. After we finish eating we'll go spend some time with 'em. They're real sociable pigs."

"Looks like they've grown since I saw you racing them at Angie's birthday party." That fateful day that had kicked off this rodeo.

"They have. They won't reach full size until they're six. They'll top out at a hundred twenty pounds or so. Pickens might not make that and Slim might overshoot the mark."

"Will you still race them?"

"Heck, yeah. They live for racing." He chuckled. "Me, too. I can still lift 'em into the back of the truck, but I'm building them a ramp. Don't want to give myself a hernia trucking them over to Mom's for parties."

Dallas had finished half his sandwich when he heard a cooing sound through the open window of the house. He glanced at Beau. "Is that—"

"Yep, that's my baby girl." He found room on the small table for his sandwich plate and stood. "Go ahead and finish your sandwich. I'll need to change her before I bring her out."

After he went through the back door, Dallas settled back and tucked into his sandwich. The setting was peaceful, but not silent. Birds twittered in the pines and aspen behind the house. Small animals rustled in the underbrush and the pigs snuffled and grunted down in their pen.

Inside the house Beau talked to Maverick, his voice mellow and loving. She talked back, giggling and throwing out random syllables that would become words when she was a few months older.

A relaxing warmth moved through his body, relaxing his tense muscles. This was the life for him, a place on the ranch, Angie by his side, and the prospect of a family in the future. It was within reach, as long as it didn't blow up in his face.

26

When her mom's house came into view, Angie sucked in a breath. "Tyra and Jess are here."

"If your mom invited them, I'd say she's figured it out, or at least most of it."

"Good guess. Penny's not here, though, and neither are Ella or Molly. Could that mean that Sky, Marsh and Bret aren't in on it?"

"I can believe Sky and Marsh aren't. But Gil and Bret are so close." Kendall parked the truck. "Surely they've talked about it."

"Maybe he didn't feel the need to show up since Gil spoke for both of them."

"Maybe." Kendall opened her door. "Remind me when we get back to move the seat back a notch. I'm squishing little whoozit."

"Will do." Angie got out and walked with her to the porch steps. "By the way, are you and Cheyenne ever gonna name that kid?"

"It's not that easy when Penny's due around the same time. Cheyenne and I got together with Penny and Sky last weekend to compare our list of favorites so we don't unknowingly choose the same one."

"Wow, I didn't think of that. Is anybody planning to use the name Desiree?"

"It's on the list, but more likely for a middle than a first. I might use my mother's for a middle. But first names... we can't decide."

"Sounds complicated."

"More than I ever expected. What if we let Penny and Sky have a name and they announce it? Then two weeks later we're hit with buyer's remorse? Or I guess it would be namer's remorse."

"I can see why your bambino is nameless." She crossed the porch and opened the door for Kendall. "Might as well name her after me and be done with it."

"It's on both our lists."

"Yeah?" She beamed. "That's so cool. I was kidding, but knowing I'm in the running is—"

"You're here. Thank goodness." Her mother rushed down the hall, Sam on her heels. "We've all decided that you two know something you're not telling us."

Angie looked at Kendall. "You called it."

She shrugged. "Can't get ahead of your mom."

"I was slow on the uptake on this one. I had to go back through the pictures from the birthday party to confirm my suspicions. Get on in there and tell us all." She made shooing motions with both hands while Sam danced around giving out little woofs of excitement.

Angie paused to bury her fingers in his ruff and gave him some love as her mom and Kendall headed to the living room. Dallas liked Sam a lot.

She'd overheard him say a firefighter's life didn't have room for a dog, but if—

"Angie, c'mon!"

"On my way." The dining table, positioned at one end of the large living room, held bowls and platters of food along with a pitcher of lemonade and one of iced tea. Tyra and Jess sat on the far side, napkins still folded, plates unused.

When Kendall took a seat on the other side and Angie sat next to her, her mom claimed her customary place at the head of the table, lifted a platter of sandwiches and passed it to Tyra.

Marybeth popped up from her place at the other end of the table and handed Kendall a large bowl of potato salad. "Here you go, honey."

Kendall eyed the bowl. "Hot dog. Do you have more? I don't want to be greedy, but I—"

"There's plenty more. Take what you want."

"Yum." She dished herself a generous portion.

Angie glanced across at Tyra and Jess. "Did you have to make up a story about why you were coming over?"

"Not me. Clint's at the Buffalo." Tyra gestured to her haphazard blonde updo. "Please excuse my Sunday-at-home look. Didn't bother to fix myself up, just jumped in the truck."

"I told Beau that Desiree and I had to coordinate Maverick's party," Jess said. "He's probably questioning my sanity. And I'm definitely questioning his." She glanced at Kendall. "Is Cheyenne wigging out, too?"

"As much as he's capable of since he's not prone to it." Kendall sat next to Angie. "I pretend not to notice. I have bigger fish to fry."

"Oooo, Kendall's pissed." Jess's eyes widened. "Somebody better watch out."

"I'm also hungry as a hibernating bear, so would anyone be offended if I start eating? I promise not to talk with my mouth full."

"Let's save the serious discussion until after we have some food," Angie said. "Kendall's been working like a trouper. She and bunny boo-boo need nourishment."

"Good idea." Her mom sent a glance Sam's direction. "Go lie down, Sam." The collie lingered by the table. "I mean it." With a doggy sigh, he trotted over to his bed and flopped down.

"I was famished all the time, too," Jess said. "Only I craved burgers. Burgers and shakes, especially the shakes Beau whips up. Now they don't interest me, but they might if I get pregnant again."

"Are you planning to?" Angie thought Maverick needed a brother or sister but then again, she'd have two more girls around in a few months.

"I am. That's why I'm keeping my hair short like Kendall's. I just have to convince Beau that Mav would love a sister or brother."

"He'll come around," Marybeth said. "He'll soon see that Maverick needs someone her size to play with."

"She'll have my kiddo." Kendall patted her stomach. "And Penny's. But it's not the same as a sibling. I'm planning on at least two. I would have loved a brother or sister."

"It's good to have siblings. Even when they're a pain in the butt." Angie made a face.

"I'm an only, like Kendall and Jess," her mom said. "I absolutely agree about siblings." She laughed. "Some might say I took it to extremes."

"Not me." She smiled at her mother. "If you hadn't, I wouldn't be here."

"I seriously doubt I'll have as many as you, Desiree," Jess said. "But what's a good number?"

That started a discussion that lasted through most of the meal. After Angie polished off her sandwich, she glanced over at Kendall. "I think it's time. Do you want to start?"

"I think you should. At the beginning, with your party."

"Aha!" Her mom snapped her fingers. "You flirted with Dallas."

"Yes, ma'am."

"Can't believe I missed it, but I discovered photographic evidence." She met Angie's gaze. "Then what?"

Taking a breath, she revealed her long-term plan, beginning not with the party, but instead with the bachelor auction.

Her mom's expressive eyes widened with surprise followed by an obvious moment of clarity. "So that's what Smoky was all about."

She nodded. "And it was all going as I hoped. Then he did an about-face." Now that she understood why he did, she saw no reason to describe that moment in detail.

But her mother must have guessed it was painful, judging from the sadness and regret in her eyes. "I'm so sorry," she murmured. "I wish you'd told me."

"I wish I had, too. Especially now that I know the truth behind his actions." She turned to Kendall. "Your turn."

"Before I start, Desiree, please know that I was ignorant of all this."

"Not even the part about the bachelor auction?"

"No, ma'am. I didn't find out about her interest in Dallas until I overheard him talking with my darling husband Friday morning, the day of the leak."

"Go on." Her eyes narrowed. "I take it this is the key element."

"Yes."

While Kendall described what she'd heard, Tyra, Jess, and Marybeth grew increasingly agitated. Tyra's breathing picked up and Jess clutched her glass of lemonade as if she'd like to throw it at someone. Marybeth folded her napkin into tighter and tighter squares, her jaw clenched.

Angie glanced at her mom, expecting a similar reaction. Her mom, though, remained calm. After an initial sigh of disappointment, she grew thoughtful. Eventually, though, her contemplative expression changed into a familiar steely gaze Angie hadn't seen in years. The calm before the storm.

Compassion took her by surprise, spearing her heart with a twinge of regret. Her brothers were in trouble. Big trouble.

Kendall wrapped up her portion. "Once I told Angie what I'd heard, we decided not to confront Cheyenne and instead let him and whoever was in this with him dig themselves a deeper hole. Which they did." She looked over at Angie. "I'm not sure how much you want to tell beyond that."

She wasn't sure, either. "Well, I..." She met her mom's gaze. The secret affair had seemed bold and daring, but—

"I hope you informed Dallas."

"I did."

"And how did he react?"

Damn it, she was blushing.

"Ahhh." Her mother smiled. "That tells me all I need to know. Good for you. I would have done the same."

She relaxed. Sometimes she forgot that her mother had a bold and daring streak a mile wide.

"How many of my boys are involved in this business, or I should say, in your business?"

"Besides Cheyenne, there's Clint, Beau and Gil, for sure. Those are the three who showed up on Saturday and made an opportunity to take Dallas aside to make sure he was with the program."

"Not Bret?"

"We don't know where he stands. It seems unlikely he doesn't know about it. My guess is that Lucky and Rance weren't included."

"Probably because they wouldn't have gone along with it. What about Marsh and Sky?"

Angie shrugged. "I don't know."

"If Sky's in on it," Kendall said. "Then I guarantee Penny doesn't know. I'm in touch with her a lot these days, and she would have jumped on this with both feet. She and Sky went through something similar with the guys at the Buckskin Ranch. She'd have no patience with this maneuver."

"Ella wouldn't go for it, either," Jess said. "So if Marsh is part of it, she doesn't know. Same with Molly and Bret. Molly wouldn't stand for this nonsense. Bottom line, I vote we call a family meeting tonight. Even better, let's include the Wenches."

"I'm for that," Tyra said. "Clint has some explaining to do. The sooner, the better."

"All four of those boys have explaining to do." Marybeth was spitting nails. "A family meeting is just the place for a reckoning."

"I agree a family meeting is in order." Her mother glanced around the table. "But not tonight. I have more thinking to do, more info to gather. Jess, your suggestion of bringing in the Wenches is a good one. You and I could discuss this with them and get some suggestions before we take action."

"I'll buy that," Marybeth said. "Then how about a family meeting tomorrow night?"

"That's no good, either. I'm as eager to get this settled as you are, but those boys go on duty Tuesday morning. I'm sure this situation has messed with their concentration and it's dangerous for a firefighter to work while distracted. Creating a dramatic showdown the night before they head to the firehouse would be irresponsible."

"I thought of that, too," Kendall said. "We should wait until they're off-duty and have some time to process before they go back to work."

Angie nodded. "I'm with Mom and Kendall. I'm upset with my meddling brothers, but I don't want to stress Cheyenne when it could affect his performance on the job."

"Also..." Her mom's eyes sparkled. "That gives you and Dallas two more nights to get acquainted."

"Oo-la-la." Jess grinned. "But I want to know how they're pulling it off. This family's on that road all times of the day and night. We notice whose truck is parked where."

"Yeah, Angie. I estimate Clint will be coming home around ten tonight. If your truck is parked at Dallas's place—"

"Or his is parked at Angie's," Jess said. "It would be noticed by somebody and reported on."

Kendall smiled. "They cut across the back on foot."

Angie felt another blush coming on, especially when her mom started laughing.

"That's so like you. Even as a little girl you had a devious streak. You—"

"For your information, it was Kendall's idea."

"Then here's to Kendall." Her mom raised her glass of lemonade. "Well done."

"That's what friends are for."

"Okay, let's sum up," Jess said. "We'll spend this next week planning our next move. Is that right, Desiree?"

"That's what I have in mind. I'll see if the Wenches can come over tomorrow night."

"Can we say we're continuing to coordinate Maverick's birthday party?"

"Might as well work that angle again."

"Beau's gonna think we're orchestrating the birthday party of the century. Serves him right. It irks me that I have to play nice, though. Tyra, you'll have to do the same with Clint."

"I will, for the good of the order, but something tells me I'll be too exhausted for any nighttime activities. Tonight or in the near future."

Jess nodded. "Same here. I feel a permanent headache coming on."

"I've been pulling that routine ever since Friday." Kendall winked at Angie. "Have fun for the rest of us, okay?"

Cheeks warm, Angie flashed them all a grin. "I'll do my best."

27

Dallas hadn't spent much time with little kids recently now that his younger siblings had become adults. Like the McLintocks, they were taking their time finding partners. So far, no adorable little nieces and nephews had arrived on the home front in New Jersey.

He'd forgotten how cute and funny babies could be. When you combined a red-haired little chickadee like Maverick with Beau McLintock and two pot-bellied pigs, you had a party going on.

"Okay, baby girl." Beau carried her down to the pen. "We're gonna show Uncle Dallas a *gen-u-wine* piggyback ride."

Uncle Dallas. First time anybody had called him that. He liked it.

Opening the gate, Beau motioned him into the pen. "I need you to take Jess's position." He fished in his pocket and brought out a handful of nuggets. "The starting line's at this end of the pen. The pigs take turns and Slim goes first. I need you to stand at the other end, and when we get to you, give Slim a treat."

"Got it." He shoved the nuggets in his pocket and headed for the finish line.

Slim had already lined up at the opposite end of the pen and Pickens sat behind him. Clearly those pigs knew the routine.

Positioning himself behind Slim, Beau lowered Maverick's diaper-clad bottom to the pig's back and hunched down, maintaining a firm grip on her. "And we're off!" Maverick giggled and her daddy whooped, his rapid shuffle step keeping pace with Slim's rapid trot. Beau lost his hat and kept on going.

Dallas laughed himself silly. As Beau whisked Maverick up in his arms and ran back to where Pickens waited, Slim dropped to his haunches and gazed up at Dallas.

Catching his breath, he peered down at the pig. "What do you—"

"The treat, Armstrong! The treat!"

"Oh! Sorry!" He gave Slim two to make up for it. Then he pulled out another one as Beau, Maverick and Pickens charged toward him, making him crack up again.

Beau lasted through an impressive number of laps, but eventually he started huffing and puffing. Maverick showed no signs of wanting to quit, so Dallas volunteered to trade places.

"You won't regret it, buddy. This is the thrill of a lifetime."

"I can see that." He took Maverick, whose face was pink with excitement as she babbled away. When she finished up with *huh-huh-huh* in a perfect imitation of the pigs, he lost it. Again.

Beau grinned. "Told you."

"I might have to get me one of these."

"A pig?"

"A kid."

Beau's eyes widened.

"But not anytime soon."

"Gotcha." Beau looked relieved. Poor guy was really wound up about the issue.

Dallas made sure he had a firm grip on Maverick before hunching over and settling her on Pickens' silky black and white coat. She immediately started to giggle.

"And we're off!"

Pickens responded. So did he, but the shuffle step was just as hard as it looked. He didn't manage to add the whooping part until the second lap with Slim. Staying bent over while holding tight to Maverick wasn't so simple, either. But damn, it was fun. Worth the crick developing in his back.

They were still at it when Jess came out the back door and walked down to the pen.

"Break time!" Beau called out. "Mommy's here!"

Maverick certainly knew the meaning of that. She twisted in Dallas's arms and made cooing noises as she reached in Jess's direction.

"I see Beau roped you into the piggyback ride attraction." Unlatching the gate, she stepped inside.

"No roping required. I had a great time."

"Obviously so did she." Jess smiled at her daughter. "Come tell me all about it, cutie-pie." Lifting the baby into her arms, she ruffled Maverick's curls, which were about the same length as Jess's.

Beau walked over. "How was lunch?"

"Great, as always."

"Did you get Mav's ginormous birthday party under control?"

"We made progress. Still more to do, though."

"Heaven help us all. I'm glad you've left me out of it."

"Don't worry. We have plans for you. You're not off the hook."

Dallas had to look away during that exchange. He'd never been accused of having a poker face.

Jess balanced Maverick on her hip. "Are you guys about done here?"

"I'd say so. Dallas, you ready to quit and grab another beer?"

"Yeah, I'm ready to call it." If Jess was home, chances were good Angie was, too. And he'd promised to cook dinner for her. "I'll take a raincheck on the beer, though."

Beau nodded. "Then I'll run you back home."

"You know what, Beau?" Jess glanced at him. "Let me do it. Mav's wound up from the piggyback rides and taking her for a drive always calms her down."

"Good idea. I'll go grab a shower. After this morning, I've got tile dust in my armpits." He grinned at Dallas. "I'll bet you do, too, buddy. Since tomorrow's an all-day job, you'll probably end up with tile dust in places where the sun don't shine."

"That's what showers are for. And I really appreciate your help with the tile." That much was true. Saved Angie and Kendall some work.

"Don't mention it. See you in the morning. I'm off to sweeten myself up for my lady. See you in the morning." He took the back porch steps two at a time.

"Dallas, do you need to fetch anything from the house before we take off?"

"No, ma'am."

"Then we can just walk around the house to my car."

"What about your keys?"

Transferring Maverick to her other hip, she pulled them out of her jeans pocket and lowered her voice. "Kept them in case I was able to accomplish this hat trick. I wanted a chance to talk to you when Beau's not around."

"Sounds like you heard the story over lunch."

"Yep." She started walking. "And I'm extremely put out with Beau. I can't imagine what's gotten into him. If this is a preview of how he'll act when Mav gets old enough to date… in fact, I plan to bring that up with him once the issue goes public."

"Was anything decided about that?"

"Only that nothing will happen until after you and Cheyenne come home from your next shift. Desiree wants time to consider all the angles. She doesn't want a blowup right before you two go on duty."

"I'd hoped for sooner, but I guess that makes sense. I can't predict how Cheyenne will react. I'm willing to shake hands and move on, but I don't know about him."

"I hope he would, too, but who knows?"

"Let me get the door." Lengthening his stride, he opened it and stepped away.

"Thanks." She buckled Maverick into the carrier mounted in the back seat.

After getting her door, too, he rounded the front of the car and climbed in. "What about Beau? How will he react?"

"He hates drama. He'll probably try to make it into a joke." She started the car and pulled out. "Which it is. I can't imagine how any of the guys are justifying this behavior. Did he share his position on it?"

"He thinks I appeal to Angie because I'm seven years older and she's looking for a father figure."

"What the hell?" Jess gave him a shocked glance before returning her attention to the road. "That's ridiculous. If you were twenty years older, then maybe, but seven?"

"I'm just reporting what he said."

"Well, he's sadly mistaken about his sister. She's one of the most mature and self-sufficient women I know, as evidenced by the successful business she's created. She's not looking for a *father figure*. That's BS."

"I agree."

"So that's it? The age difference?"

"He's also worried about her getting pregnant with the wrong guy."

She groaned. "I suppose he would, but that's a risk we all take if we have sex, isn't it? Did he tell you about the Midnight caper?"

"Yes, ma'am."

"That's a one-in-a-million situation."

"I realize that. What it boils down to, probably for all of them, is that our relationship could go south and impact everyone on the ranch. They're not wrong. It could."

"In Beau's case, that's the pot calling the kettle black. I hate to think what life would be like around here if he hadn't come to his senses."

"Maybe that's why he's nervous about Angie and me getting together."

"Maybe." She pulled up to his cabin and glanced toward the back seat. "Good. She conked out."

He opened the door quietly. "Thanks for the—"

"Wait a sec. I need to ask you something."

He paused and looked at her.

"The Wenches are meeting tomorrow night to discuss the situation. Desiree texted me right before I came out to the pig pen."

"Her book club? Why would she—"

"They're more than a book club. They're her closest friends. My mom was a Wench and they were kind enough to give me her spot."

"Right. I figured that out when you were one of the elves at the Christmas craft fair."

"Yeah, that was fun. Anyway, Desiree wants you and Angie to come. I told her you were still at my house and if I had a chance, I'd urge you to do it. They're meeting at seven."

"Won't that alert Angie's brothers?"

"We'll find a way to smuggle you in and out. Obviously it's up to you whether you agree to go or not, but I hope you will."

"Did Desiree contact Angie?"

"Yes, and Angie said she'd talk it over with you."

"Then we'll do that and let Desiree know."

"Those ladies are good problem solvers."

"Sounds good to me." He smiled. "Again, thanks for the ride. And the support."

"You're welcome. Have a nice evening."

"Yes, ma'am. I'm looking forward to it."

Jess chuckled. "So's she."

And didn't he love hearing that.

_**28**_

Angie had just finished talking with her mother when Dallas sent a text.

Come over around 6:30. Bring your appetite.

Angie texted back. *Which one?*

Both.

She shivered in anticipation. Jess and Tyra had promised to keep tabs on their husbands and prevent any surprise visits or disruptive phone calls. Kendall would take charge of keeping Cheyenne at home all evening, which only left Gil.

He didn't seem quite as dedicated to the cause as the other three, so she doubted he'd show up unannounced at Dallas's place tonight. Which meant they'd have the cabin to themselves.

She sent him another text. *I have champagne. Will that go with what you're making?*

Everything goes with champagne. Where did you get it?

From my mom.

Wow.

Yeah, wow was right. She'd been surprised and delighted when her mom had offered the pricey bottle.

Over coffee and dessert after lunch, the discussion had turned to the chain of events that had brought them to this point — Kendall's determination to woo and win Cheyenne, which resulted in Dallas moving into Cheyenne's vacated cabin.

Angie had announced it was the hand of Fate confirming that Dallas was destined to be her happy-ever-after guy. That statement had prompted her mom to give her the champagne currently chilling in her fridge. If her brothers hadn't blocked her plans in February....

But they had, mucking up what might have been a smooth transition from friendship to something more. They didn't trust her to make good choices, damn it. Infuriating, but hurtful, too. Would they stick to their guns when confronted? Would her pushback be successful or cause a rift in the family?

Not the questions she'd dwell on tonight, though. She'd wash off those cares, along with the residue from a morning of tiling, and arrive at Dallas's back door eager for a sexy, romantic evening. They'd drink champagne compliments of her mom, who absolutely believed in Fate and in her, which was gratifying.

At six-twenty-three, wearing a silky black tank and shorts outfit exactly like the white one from the night before, she shoved her arms it the sleeves of her parka. The combo had made an impression the night before, so why not stay with what worked?

Snow boots still made the most sense and she liked the sensation of the fur lining on her bare toes. Tucking the champagne in a wine bag, she set out for a rendezvous with Dallas.

She had to admit sneaking over there added spice to their meeting. Technically she had her brothers to thank for that. But since she didn't plan to give them any space in her world tonight, she'd skip thanking them, too.

The sun was still up, although soon it would dip behind the Sapphires as the shadow of the mountains created an early twilight. The major curve in the road gave Dallas's front porch a view of those mountains at sunset, but they wouldn't dare sit out there. For now, they were better off staying in.

She breathed in the fragrance of pine, wild grass and the delicate scent of the first wildflowers. Even though Dallas had only taken this route a few times, his boots had left a faint path and she followed it.

Soon the scent of the forest blended with the aroma of cedar smoke. Would they eat in front of his fireplace tonight? Her body hummed in anticipation of his kisses, his embrace, his... yeah, that. She walked faster.

A plume of smoke rose from the trees, a feathery gray against a translucent pale blue sky. Breaks in the foliage gave her a glimpse of the warm brown logs of his cabin.

Her heart thumped and she grew short of breath. The stairs that led up to his back door were only yards away. Then the door flew open.

Dallas clattered down the steps, lengthening his stride as he hurried toward her, his smile wide. "I was watching for you."

"And here I am." She walked faster, straight into his open arms.

"Here you are." His voice was husky as he pulled her close with one hand and relieved her of the wine bag with the other. "Longest afternoon ever." His mouth captured hers in a hot kiss that curled her toes into the fur of her snow boots.

Thrusting his tongue deep, he ravished her mouth until she had to cling to him or lose her balance. Clutching the front of his soft shirt, she burrowed against him, wanting… needing….

He broke away from the kiss with a groan. "If I don't… stop…" He dragged in a breath. "Dinner's gonna be… ruined…." Dipping his head, he closed his eyes, coming back for more.

She let go of his shirt and clamped her hand over his mouth. "We're going in."

His dark lashes lifted, revealing the heat simmering in his magnetic gaze.

Her body clenched in eager response. "We're not ruining dinner." Her words were breathy, but firmly delivered. "Not on my watch."

A flicker of amusement replaced the seductive glow in his eyes. His chest heaved. Then he gently removed her hand. "Understood." Then he placed a kiss in her palm. "Raincheck."

"You know it, mister."

He chuckled and wrapped his arm around her waist. "Yeah, I do." He started toward the back steps, tucking her in beside him, matching his stride to hers. "I tell myself that this can all wait at least until after we eat, but I catch sight of you and *whoosh*, I go up in flames."

"I know the feeling."

"Happy to hear it." When they reached the steps, he ushered her ahead of him. "Wore my favorite boots, I see. Got something white under that parka?"

"Nope."

He gulped. "You came over here na—"

"Hell, no. I have my limits." She walked through the door he'd left open in his rush to get to her. "Something smells steak-a-licious."

"Which means we broke up the party just in time." He came in and closed the door. "If you can smell it, we're ready to eat. But first, let me take your coat. My curiosity is killing me."

"Can't have that." She turned, backed up a few paces and unzipped her parka. "Ta-da!" She whipped it off with a flourish and handed it to him.

He took it, but his attention stayed glued to her black nightwear. "Hot damn." He sucked in a breath. "How do you feel about cold steak sandwiches?"

"I'd rather have mine hot and juicy, please."

"Hm." Hanging her coat on a hook without looking, he moved a step closer, a sexy smile curving his kissable mouth.

She shook her head and backed up. "I'm sure you had a plan."

"Plans are made to be changed." Reaching for the knob on the stove, he twisted it to off.

"Give me a job. I can help you with this feast."

"Everything's done."

"There's *nothing* I can do?"

He sighed. "Yes, ma'am, there is. You can take your tempting self into the living room and sit at the table. If you hang around wearing that black silky stuff, all I can think of is—"

"Which was the point of wearing it, but I didn't mean to sabotage the dinner you worked so hard to fix. I'm sorry."

"Don't be. I love that you wore that outfit for me. But if you don't leave the kitchen, I'm liable to drop our steaks on the floor. Considering the condition of the floor, they'd become inedible, even if we rinsed them in the bathroom sink."

She glanced around. "Good point. It's a wonder you managed to fix this meal with no sink in here and the counters filled with pots and pans. I probably should have suggested my place."

"I wanted you here."

"You did? Why?"

"For a solid year I've fantasized you in this cabin, over by the fire, but mostly in my bed..." He cleared his throat. "Better vamoose."

"Okay." She turned and fled into the living room, a place so familiar from countless visits when Cheyenne lived in this cabin.

He'd left his furniture when he'd moved in with Kendall, taking only his bed, which he'd claimed was bigger than hers. This morning the room had looked much the same except for the table and chairs they'd moved out of the kitchen in preparation for laying tile.

It didn't look the same now. Dallas had done more than cook dinner. He'd rearranged the living room, turning it into a romantic setting that touched her so deeply her throat tightened.

She'd placed two candles on her dining table. He'd put them everywhere. Candles and the crackling logs on the hearth provided the only light in the room. The guy wasn't intimidated by fire or afraid of candles. *I go up in flames.* He was heat and light, aglow with a fierce passion for life. She'd found the one.

<u>29</u>

Angie's gasp of surprise and pleasure was exactly what Dallas had been going for. He'd bought a slew of tea lights back in February, figuring he'd want some atmosphere if he'd be entertaining Angie. Finally, it was happening.

He'd moved the small kitchen table over behind the couch and put a chair on either side so they could eat and see the fire like they had at her place. He'd started out with the lamps on and a few tea lights. Not quite right.

The lamps weren't on a dimmer switch. They were too bright, but the room would be very dark without them. Unless....

More tea lights helped. On a roll, he'd pressed all sorts of glass containers into service—drinking glasses, wine glasses, shot glasses, saucers, jelly jars and their lids.

He'd emptied the boxes and lit them all in advance. Running out to meet her and lingering to indulge himself with kisses hadn't been the brightest idea. But he'd wanted to make a splash.

"Like it?" he called out as he forked their filets onto dinner plates.

"Love it."

The emotion in her voice triggered a rush of happiness that warmed him all over, and not in a sexual way. No question her nightwear got him hot. He'd been ready to grab her hand and head for the bedroom.

Thankfully she'd put the skids on that program. He would have wasted the opportunity to show her how he felt — about her, about being gifted with a night alone, about the importance he placed on the chance to welcome her into his house.

"You must have used every glass in the cupboard. Do you have any left for the champagne?"

"Yes, ma'am." He slid a twice-baked potato onto each plate, nudging over the grilled asparagus to make room. "I kept out two wine glasses because I have a bottle of red. Champagne's better, though." He carried the plates into the living room.

She was wandering around the room peering at the flickering tea lights. Glancing up, she met his gaze. "This is awesome. What made you think of it?"

"You."

"I remind you of a bunch of tiny tea lights?"

He smiled and set the plates on his red-and-white checkered tablecloth. "You don't consider that a compliment?"

"I guess it is, sort of. A little vague."

Laughing, he crossed the room and took her in his arms. "How about... you make me feel like I swallowed a bunch of tea lights. How's that?"

"Terrible." She grinned. "I picture a tortured guy on a commercial for antacids. Try again."

He gazed into her sparkling blue eyes. "I'd say *you light up my life* but that's so overdone."

"No, it's not. I love that song."

I love you. Perfect opening. Too early. "Me, too."

She reached up and stroked his cheek. "You shaved."

"I should hope so. Bristles would cancel out tea lights."

"You put in a lot of effort. Thank you."

"You're welcome." If he kissed her now, he'd land right back where he'd been a few minutes ago. "Ready to open the champagne and eat that steak?"

"Yes."

He released her. "Have a seat. I'll get the bottle and the glasses."

When he returned, she was safely ensconced in the left-hand chair. He placed a glass at each place and peeled the foil from a very pricey bottle of champagne. "Your mom goes big."

She glanced up at him. "Now she does, but she couldn't when Sky and Beau were little. By the time I came along, she could splurge on herself and on me. Or so I was told."

"You don't remember getting lots of stuff?"

"Nope. She quit before I became spoiled beyond belief."

"That leaves plenty of room for me to spoil you."

"Oh?"

"But not with stuff. I have other methods in mind."

"I like the sound of that." Her eyes glowed as she touched her glass to his. "To us."

His breath caught. "To us." He held her gaze as he took a sip.

Slowly she lowered her glass. "Clearly you like making people happy. No wonder you went along with Cheyenne's program."

"Learned a hard lesson, though. Making him happy almost cost me...a lot."

She set down her champagne and picked up her fork and steak knife. "Have you ever meddled in your little sister's love life?"

"No, but I would have. My other sister, who's two years younger than me, threatened major repercussions." He waited to start until she'd tried the steak.

"I like her already." She cut a piece, put it in her mouth and hummed with approval. Then she gave him a thumbs-up.

Laughing, he dug in. "Glad you like it."

"Mm-hm." After chewing and swallowing the bite of steak, she tasted the potato and the asparagus, raving about both.

While they continued to eat, she pumped him for info about what spices he used. "Not that I plan to jump into cooking mode, but I could beef up the spice drawer at my house so you have a better array."

"Is that a hint?"

"That's a freaking flashing billboard. You're welcome to cook in my kitchen anytime. And I have a sink."

"I have great memories of your sink." He refilled their champagne glasses.

Color bloomed in her cheeks. "So do I, Patrick — I mean *Dallas.*"

"Very funny."

"Which reminds me. How come your New Jersey parents gave you a cowboy name? Did they know in advance you'd become one?"

"My mom and dad were newlyweds when they attended an insurance conference in Dallas. I was conceived there."

"I'll be darned. Do you think your name influenced your decision to come out West?"

"Might have. I've always known it's a cowboy name, which suited me just fine."

"They have plenty of cowboys in Texas, too. Why not go there?"

"I also love mountains. I searched online for rural fire departments near mountain ranges. Wagon Train was the first one I found with an opening."

"Lucky me."

"And lucky me." The fire was slowly dying. He glanced at her plate. She was about half finished. Might as well leave the fire alone.

"How come a caravan of girlfriends didn't follow you out here from New Jersey?"

"I didn't give any of them a reason to."

"Then you must not have cooked them a steak."

"Or anything else, for that matter."

"Really? She blinked in surprise. "Why not?"

"For the same reason you dated guys from out of town. I didn't want to get serious about somebody until I had my life sorted out." He smiled. "And cooking for someone is serious business."

Candlelight flickered in her eyes as she held his gaze. "I plan to eat every bite of this terrific meal. But for the record, I feel like crawling across this table and kissing you right now."

"Save that thought. And FYI, I ran out of time, so we don't have dessert."

"Oh, yes, we do." She gave him a sultry glance.

His blood heated. "I stand corrected."

"You sure are sexy when you get that gleam in your eye."

"Backatcha."

"Torn between eating delicious food and getting naked with the man who made it. What a dilemma." She scooped out the last of the potato and licked it off the fork.

"You're doing that on purpose."

"Yes, I am."

He shifted in his chair to ease the pinch in his jeans and continued eating. They were both almost done.

"Tight quarters over there?"

"I can handle it."

"It'd be more fun if you'd let me."

"Hey."

She smiled. "Just looking forward to dessert." She finished off her asparagus. Only a little bit of steak was left on her plate.

He cleaned his and swallowed the rest of his champagne. A small amount was left in the bottle. He lifted it. "Want more?"

"Yes, thank you."

"Tell me when."

"I'll take all of it."

He emptied the bottle into her glass. She was up to something. But what?

After she'd polished off the rest of her steak, she took a sip of champagne and settled back in her chair. "What an amazing meal. Thank you."

"Anytime."

She glanced at the fire. "It's died down."

"Yes, ma'am."

"Let's clear these plates." She scooted back from the table. "I'm ready for dessert."

Which didn't fit with her request for the last of the champagne. "I'll get the dishes. Just sit and enjoy the fire."

"Okay."

He stacked the dishes next to the stove. They could wait until morning. Returning to the living room, he circled the area, blowing out the tea lights, his body hot and achy with need.

After he'd extinguished the last candle, the fire's orange glow provided just enough light to keep him from running into something as he went back to the table.

Angie stood, her champagne glass in hand.

"You can just leave that on the table."

"I'm not finished. I saved some to go with my dessert."

Whatever she had in mind, he was in. He held out his hand. "Then come to bed."

30

Angie let Dallas tug off his boots and socks. But after that she took over, leaving her champagne on the nightstand while she began the mouthwatering task of divesting this beautiful man of his clothes.

"Don't take too long."

The urgency in his plea fired her up even more. "I won't. But I've wanted to do this ever since the auction." She quickly unbuttoned his cuffs and started down his shirtfront. Leaning forward, she inhaled a woodsy scent blended with the musk of arousal. "You smell so good."

His chest heaved. "Not as good as you, peppermint lady."

Yanking his shirt out of the waistband of his jeans, she pushed it over his broad shoulders to reveal the muscled chest sprinkled with dark hair that had captivated her more than a year ago. Her nipples grew taut just looking at that magnificent display.

"You're lingering."

She lifted her head and met the intensity burning in his dark eyes. "I'm reliving the moment you came out on stage. I was a goner."

"Wish I'd known you were there."

She shook her head. "Wrong place, wrong time."

"And speaking of time...."

She held his gaze as she fumbled with his belt buckle. "I'm getting there."

He gave her a crooked smile. "It'll go faster if you watch what you're doing."

"True." She focused on getting the buckle open. The metal button was easy. She pulled down his zipper carefully, mindfully. Didn't want to pinch anything valuable and it could happen the way she was quivering.

Hooking her thumbs in the waistband of his briefs, she took a deep breath and pulled them down along with his jeans. Aided by the weight of his belt, they slid to the floor without her help. Thank goodness, since she'd focused all her attention on the treasures she'd unveiled.

He stepped out, his breathing ragged. "I need to get a—"

"Not yet." She struggled to get the words out. "I have... plans." Glancing up, she motioned toward the bed. "Lie down. On your back."

He frowned. "I'll still need—"

"Later." She ran her tongue over her lips. He should get that message.

His brow cleared and his breath hitched. "Oh." Another quick breath. A flare of excitement in his eyes. "But I'm not gonna come."

"We'll see." Whipping her tank over her head and shimmying out of her shorts, she dropped them on the pile of clothes lying on the floor.

He tossed the thick Pendleton blanket to a nearby chair as if it weighed nothing. Throwing back the covers, he stretched out on the white sheet — six feet three and a half inches, two hundred and twenty-five pounds of gloriously aroused male.

She'd obtained those stats months ago. Eavesdropping was an art.

He turned his head in her direction as she picked up her champagne and took a sip. The article she'd read had said that was plenty.

When he raised his eyebrows, she pressed a finger to her lips. A tight seal was critical. She'd rather not spew champagne all over him and his clean sheets.

Straddling his thighs, she leaned down, pressed her mouth to the tip of his cock and wrapped her fingers around the base. He shuddered and clenched his fists, his chest rising and falling faster.

Slowly, carefully, her lips tight, she took his pride and joy as far as she dared, about halfway. Hollowing her cheeks, she put that bubbly into action.

He gasped, then moaned.

She increased the speed, the fizzy sensation tickling her tongue. Had to be having the same effect on him, judging from the way he'd started to shake.

Muttering curses under his breath, he squeezed his eyes shut, pounded the mattress with both fists and groaned.

Time to raise the stakes. Reaching between his thighs, she cupped his family jewels and began a slow massage.

He hissed her name through clenched teeth. She responded by swallowing the champagne and taking him all the way in.

With a bellow of surrender, he erupted, warm liquid filling her mouth. She swallowed again. And again.

Gulping for air, her name a whispered chant, he trembled beneath her, his skin flushed and shiny with sweat, his eyes still closed.

He was slow to recover. She stayed right where she was until he relaxed against the mattress and uncurled his fingers.

When at last she lifted her head, his eyes were open, his gaze trained on her.

She gave him a smile. "Well?"

He started to speak. Stopped. Shook his head.

"That good? Or that bad?"

"That good." His voice rasped.

"Then you had fun."

"A rollercoaster is fun." He cleared his throat. "This was... I think I lost some brain cells. But who cares?"

"Think you'd like to do it again sometime?"

He laughed. "What a crazy question. *Yes.* But only after I've had a few days to cool down. You might have just sidelined me for the rest of the night."

"I doubt it." If so, they'd be creative. Her needs simmered just under the surface, ready to flare up the minute he touched her.

"I dunno. You got me good. If I'm down for the count I'm sorry, but you have only yourself to blame."

She smiled. "You're teasing me."

"Am I?" Mischief sparkled in his eyes.

"A little trick like that won't put you out of commission for the evening." It tickled her to hear him talk like that, though. She'd been going for memorable and obviously had achieved it.

"Let's hope you're right. How about coming down here for some cuddling? After that, I could use some R&R."

"On my way." Shifting her position, she scooted up next to him and settled into the curve of his arm, her hand resting on his lightly furred chest. "I can feel your heart beating."

He turned his head and smiled. "You gave that a workout, too. Felt like it would explode any minute."

"Okay, be honest. Too intense?"

"No." Rolling to his side, he combed his fingers through her hair as he gazed into her eyes. "It was fantastic. Incredible. Thank you for giving me such a wild experience. Did you dream it up yourself?"

"Nope. Read about it a while ago. Then Mom handed me champagne and I couldn't resist giving it a try."

"I doubt it has to be pricey champagne."

"It doesn't even have to be champagne. Anything carbonated would work."

"Champagne's classier." He gave her a slow, languorous kiss, his tongue exploring her mouth with lazy strokes.

That was all she needed to catch fire. A sweet ache built within her core, demanding attention. She snuggled closer.

He lifted his mouth a fraction. "You taste like sex."

"Fancy that."

"Gives me an idea."

"Sounds promising." The ache became more insistent.

"Stay here. I'll be right back." He left the bed, his movements agile, his pride and joy showing signs of life.

"I don't think you're compromised, mister."

"To coin a phrase, *fancy that*." He ducked into the bathroom and returned with a fluffy bath towel. "Lie on your back, please."

She stretched out.

"Lift your sexy fanny." He slipped the soft terry under her.

"I think I know where this is going."

"It's not original, and it won't have the same effect on you, but let's do it, anyway."

"Can't let good champagne go to waste." She shivered in anticipation.

"Exactly." Picking up the glass, he set it on the floor by the bed and climbed in. He started by kissing her full on the mouth. Then he began his travels, mapping her body, leaving the damp imprint of his lips and tongue wherever he went.

By the time he dipped his tongue in her navel, she was panting and hot, so hot. Moving between her thighs, he reached one long arm over the bed.

Moments later cool, fizzy liquid trickled over the epicenter of her sizzling body. She gasped in shock. "Dallas! That's—"

"Shh. I've got this." He began to lick, his warm tongue instantly raising her temperature. More champagne.

"Yikes! That's so... so... nice." She gulped as his tongue worked its magic.

More licking. More champagne. Intimate nuzzling. Teasing kisses, moving her closer, ever closer....

Almost there... tantalizingly out of reach... She moaned. "Dallas...."

Abandoning the champagne, he settled down to business. *Yes.*

She came in seconds, arching her back and making noise, lots of it. He anchored her hips with his big hands and went on loving her, driving her up again, pushing her over the brink into a dazzling whirlpool of pleasure.

When he released her, she sank back to the mattress, blissful and slightly dazed. What was that sound? A drawer opening? The rip of foil? Was he—

Yes, he was. Poised over her once again, he leaned down and captured her mouth as he slid his cock deep. Not compromised at all.

Wrapping her arms around him, she caught his rhythm, undulating with his unhurried thrusts as the coil at her center wound tighter.

He raised his head, a luminous glow in his dark eyes. "Once more."

"Yes." Her breath caught as a gentle spasm hit. "I'm going to—"

"I know." He smiled. "Me, too."

With a soft cry, she welcomed a climax that flowed over her, engulfing her in a fluid embrace. Holding her gaze, he pressed deeper, the warmth in

his eyes burrowing into her soul as he let go with a sigh, her partner in a pulsing, rippling dance.
        Perfect.

31

Dallas hadn't meant to fall asleep, but to be fair, Angie had started it. They'd been lying facing each other, talking about the Wenches and their planned meeting, when she'd drifted off.

He'd conked out soon afterward, leaving the lamp on. Good thing he'd set his alarm before she'd arrived last night or they might have blown the program. Its chime woke him from the deepest sleep he'd had in years.

She sat up, clearly disoriented. "Is it morning? Don't tell me it's morning."

"Afraid so."

Groaning, she flopped back on the pillow. "I can't believe I fell *asleep*. We had all night together and I had to go and—"

He silenced her tirade with a long, slow kiss. Worked like a charm. A little too well, in fact. In seconds they were tangled together, ready for another romp.

He drew back, breathing hard. "We can't. It's time to go."

"I know. I'm sorry that I—"

"Hey, I fell asleep right after you did. Probably for the best. Obviously we were tired and we have a big day ahead."

She sighed. "All true." Grabbing his cheeks, she gave him one more quick kiss and climbed out of bed. "Brr. My outfit doesn't seem like such a great idea this morning." She picked up her silk shorts.

Swinging his feet to the floor, he stood. "So wear my sweats."

She smiled. "Because they would fit like a glove?"

"They have cuffs and a drawstring." He crossed to the dresser, took out a pair and tossed them in her direction. "Give it a shot. Nobody will see you, anyway."

"Let's hope not. Thanks."

"I'll be glad when the secrecy is over." He gathered up his clothes and concentrated on getting dressed instead of watching Angie, a distraction he couldn't afford right now.

"Which reminds me, did we decide we're both going to the meeting with the Wenches?"

"I'm willing if you are."

"Then we'll go." She started laughing.

"What?" He looked over and was hit by a wave of lust, followed by the deeper emotion that had been filling his chest with warmth a lot recently.

"I could put two of me in these." She stood topless, head down, surveying the baggy sweats cinched around her slender waist. "At least they won't fall off."

"And oh, how I want them to."

She glanced up. "These sweats turn you on?"

"Not the sweats. But you wearing them? Yes, ma'am. Never could resist cute *and* sexy. I'm officially ignoring you until we're ready to walk out the door."

"We? You don't have to go."

"It's cold out there. And still pretty dark. I feel the need to walk you home."

"Aww. That's sweet. I accept."

Moments later they set off, hand-in-hand. First time they'd held hands like lovers out for a stroll. He looked forward to doing it more often once they ditched the secrecy.

"Did you notice we've already created a path?"

"We sure have."

"It's nice, being able to walk back and forth instead of driving."

Even nicer if they stayed put in one place. But he didn't say anything. It wasn't time.

"What about tonight? My cabin or yours?"

"Yours."

"That was easy. Do you think we should trade off? Spend Friday night at yours?"

"Probably."

"It's a deal, then."

A temporary deal. He wouldn't be on board with that routine forever. But it was early days.

* * *

Pretending to be angry, or at least indifferent to Angie was growing old. Dallas couldn't wait until the day — or night — of reckoning came and her brothers discovered the romance going on under their noses.

Cheyenne showed up, along with Beau, to help with the tiling job. Marybeth and Desiree arrived around noon with another feast.

Judging from the hilarity during that lunch break, anyone would think they had a party going on. He played his part and so did Angie. They avoided eye contact and maintained their distance. He hated it.

During lunch, Desiree slipped him a note with instructions for tonight's meeting with the Wenches. The work dragged on forever, but at last the tiling was finished. He raved about it because he was supposed to. His heart wasn't in it.

After everyone left, including Angie, he grabbed a shower and headed over the now-familiar path to her back door.

She answered his light tap immediately. She'd pulled her hair into a ponytail and put on lipstick. "Did Mom give you instructions?"

He took the note out of his pocket and showed it to her. "Evidently they're planning to feed us after the discussion."

"That's the plan. Did you remember to leave lights on at your place?"

"Lights on, sound system turned up so if anyone does come to the door, they'll assume I can't hear them knocking." He gazed at the pretty pink color on her lips. Seemed like a Keep Off sign. "Since you're wearing lipstick, I suppose I—"

"Yeah, better not. Mom will be here any minute, anyway." She smiled. "Later."

He took a deep breath. "Can't wait."

"Me, either, but this is important."

"Do I really have to lie down in the back seat on the drive over? I haven't been horizontal in a back seat since—"

"Spare me the details, lover boy." She gave him a pat on the chest. "It's broad daylight and somebody could see you riding in Mom's truck. The meeting's no secret but your presence there definitely is."

"Okay, then. One other thing. I've met all the Wenches, but other than Jess and your mom, I'm not sure I can keep them straight."

"Just go by color. They'll be wearing it and their chairs will match—red for Colleen, orange for Teresa, yellow for Nancy, indigo for Annette and blue for Cindy."

"Maybe I should write that on my arm."

"You'll be fine." She cocked her head. "Mom just pulled in." She hurried out of the kitchen and headed for the front door.

He followed. "How do we work this?"

"Stay inside until I open the door to the back seat."

"Got it."

"This is one time I wish I'd located the steps in front instead of at the far end. It would be easier for you to get in without being seen." She glanced over her shoulder. "Just stay low and move fast."

He rolled his eyes. "Or I could crawl down the porch on my belly."

"Yeah, do that." She laughed. "I'd love to see it."

"Well, you're not gonna. Honest to God, Angie, this is—"

"Necessary." She opened the front door.

"Yes, ma'am."

After she went out, he stood in the doorway waiting for his cue. Desiree had pulled her purple F-350 so the passenger side faced the porch steps. Angie hurried down them, her ponytail swishing back and forth.

When she jerked open the back door and climbed in beside her mom, he took off his hat and hunkered down. Crab-walking out, he shut her door and motored down the porch, hunched over much as he'd been while giving Maverick rides on Slim and Pickens. His back reminded him it wasn't his favorite position.

Navigating the steps that way was tricky but he managed to avoid a face-plant. He hopped into the truck like a gigantic frog and closed the door.

As Desiree put the truck in gear, he stretched out on the back seat — *stretched out* being a relative term. He didn't fit. Turning on his side, he pulled up his knees in a semi-fetal pose. Marginally better.

Angie cleared her throat, no doubt trying not to crack up.

"Go ahead and laugh. Just promise you didn't video that routine."

"That would be mean."

Desiree glanced in the rearview mirror. "You're a good sport, Dallas."

"Thanks. I feel like an idiot."

"You won't have to do it again. It'll be dark when we come back."

"What about when we get to your house? What if someone happens to be down at the barn and sees me get out?"

"We're going around to my private entrance."

Private entrance? "Won't that look suspicious?"

"Not for a Wenches meeting. I'd do it even if I'd only brought Angie over. It's closer to the library. Sometimes the Wenches park back there, too."

That made no sense to him from his limited knowledge of the house. Maybe it would once they got there.

After a short ride, Desiree rolled to a stop and turned off the engine. "We're here. You can stop hiding."

He unfolded himself, sat up and looked around. Trees shielded the area and sure enough a couple of other trucks had parked there. Straight ahead was a blank wall.

Then Desiree clicked a fob on her keychain and a door-sized section of the wall swung open, spilling a shaft of light into the gathering dusk.

"Whoa."

Angie glanced into the back seat. "My dad created that. And there's more."

Dallas kept his attention on the magic door as he grabbed his hat and climbed down, his boots crunching on pine needles from the nearby trees. "What about the others? How do they get in?"

"Each of my Wenches has a key fob like mine."

"You must really trust these ladies."

"Implicitly." She got out and closed her door. "As Angie said, this is only the beginning." She led the way through the door.

He caught Angie by the shoulder, leaned down and whispered in her ear. "Is your mom a secret agent?"

"Nope." Her voice rippled with laughter. "Something way better."

32

Angie could barely contain her excitement. Although her mom probably could have smuggled Dallas into the library without revealing her secret, she'd chosen to bring him into the fold. Which meant her mother believed in this relationship. That was huge.

Dallas gestured for her to go in ahead of him. She did, but the minute he came through the door, she threaded her fingers through his.

"As you can see, Dallas," her mom began, "this is my bedroom." She swept a hand to encompass the luxurious setting.

"It's very nice." He looked bewildered. "But I don't understand why this is the shortest route to the library."

"You will." She walked through the double doors into her office. "This is where I work."

"Very convenient." He surveyed the cluttered desk, the big computer screen, and the large windows looking out into the forest. Then he quickly scanned the bookshelves. Why so many by M. R. Morrison? "I've never been clear on what you do."

Her mom smiled. "Because that's the way I wanted it. My work is a closely kept secret, known only by a few — the Wenches, Buck and Marybeth, my kids, and the people they've fallen in love with."

Angie's breath hitched. She hadn't said the word yet and neither had he. Would he think she'd told her mother before telling him? He squeezed her hand. She squeezed back. They'd talk later.

"Anyway," her mom continued, "since I can see Angie's nutty about you and you seem to be nutty about her, it's time you found out. I write Western novels under the name M. R. Morrison."

He tensed. "With all due respect, ma'am, that can't be right. I've read his books. M. R. Morrison is a guy."

"You're supposed to think that." Angie turned to him. "When Mom sold her first book more than thirty years ago, her publishers chose to market her as a guy because they believed sales would be better."

"At the time, I'm sure they were right." Her mother pointed to the copies of her books lining the shelves. "There's the result. My career took off and is still going strong. I've considered outing myself, but my agent and publisher aren't wild about the idea."

"People in town must have found out, though. I mean, you've lived here for a long—"

"They haven't found out because those who know are very good secret-keepers. Judging from everything I've observed, so are you."

He sucked in a breath. "I'm honored that you trust me with it. And I'm intimidated as hell. Pardon the language."

Her mom laughed. "Nothing wrong with a little intimidation. I used it on my kids if they showed any tendency to be blabbermouths when they were younger. Now it's second nature for them to protect the information."

"You don't have to worry about me."

"If I'd doubted that for a second, I wouldn't have told you."

"The bookstore makes a lot more sense, now, especially the great selection of M. R. Morrison titles."

"And my extensive promotions for those books are a tax write-off." She walked over to a floor-to-ceiling bookshelf. "Let's go see the Wenches."

"I'm guessing there's another secret entrance."

"Smart boy." She gave a gentle push and the bookshelves slowly began to revolve.

"My dad built that, too," Angie said.

He gave her a quick glance. "Do you have one?"

"It's on the drawing board if I decide to add on."

He murmured a soft *cool* as the bookshelf completed a one-eighty to reveal the library. And the Wenches.

They sat in rainbow order, with Colleen in red on one end and her mom's purple chair on the other. Two dining chairs meant for her and Dallas turned the rainbow into a loose circle with enough room for them to step in and sit down.

Releasing her hand, Dallas straightened his shoulders and smiled. "Good evening, ladies. Thanks for the invitation."

"We're glad you're here," Jess motioned to the wooden chairs. "Have a seat."

Dallas waited until Angie took the one next to her mother before he settled down beside Colleen.

Nancy spoke up next. "Before we get to the subject at hand, I'd like to say that it's nice getting a chance to talk to you one-on-one, Dallas."

"I think it's more like one-on-seven," Teresa said, "depending on where you fit into the count, Angie."

"I'm with Dallas, so I guess it's two-on-seven."

Nancy waved a dismissive hand. "Whatevs, as the kids say these days. Except for Jess, we've all known you since you were born, but we have precious little intel on this handsome fellow." She focused on Dallas. "It seems like we haven't seen that much of you, even though you've lived on the ranch almost a year."

"Yes, ma'am. To be honest, I've been hesitant to butt into... well, the routines everyone had established. And I'm at the fire station a lot."

"Exactly. And thank you for your service. You're a fine addition to our fire department."

"Thanks, Nancy. I love my job."

Angie gave him a quick smile. One down, only four more to ID.

"Dallas," Teresa said, "I also appreciate your contribution to the department, both on the firetruck and..." She made a twirling motion with her hand. "On the stage."

"Thank—"

"My comments included that, too, Teresa," Nancy said.

Yay. Nancy had just given him Teresa's name. Only three to go.

"Didn't sound like you were including it."

"I didn't specifically mention the bachelor auction because I didn't want Dallas to think we're sexually objectifying him."

"I wasn't sexually objectifying him."

And... the discussion was officially off the rails.

"Can't I thank him for adding to my enjoyment of that evening?"

"She really enjoyed it, Dallas," Cindy said. "I thought I might have to dump our champagne ice bucket over her head."

Teresa swung to face her. "You're one to talk. You were yelling *sock it to me, baby!*"

"Settle down, you guys," Colleen said. "The man's face is the color of my sweater. Dallas, pay no attention to them."

"Don't you pretend you weren't whooping and hollering, *Miss* Colleen." Nancy gave her the eye. "I have witnesses. Annette, back me up, here."

"Dallas, we were acting like crazy ladies that night." Annette spoke with her usual grace. "Also, Nancy's right. You've been elusive. Mysterious, even. Please forgive us for having flashbacks to the auction when you walked in just now."

"It's okay. I'm glad you all had fun."

"Angie did, too," Jess said with a wink. "We just didn't know it."

He glanced at her. "No whooping and hollering?"

Now it was her turn to blush. "I was. On the inside."

A collective *awwww* went up from the group.

"I believe we've covered that topic sufficiently." Her mom had stayed out of it, but now she took charge. "I meant for this to be a chance for everyone to get to know Dallas a little better. You've just learned he can handle public embarrassment just fine." She turned to her left. "Angie, what can you tell us about him?"

She gasped. "Me?"

"I'm sure you know him better than anyone in this room."

"Well..." Her brain whirled. "He was born in New Jersey and he comes from a large family."

"We've heard that, sweetie," Nancy said. "Tell his about his character."

He gave her an amused smile.

"Well, he's brave. By choosing to be with me, he's risking his friendship with Cheyenne, who's also his work buddy. He could lose the house he's hoping to buy. He's also funny, and tender, and a great cook."

"Damn, girl." Cindy shook her head hard enough to wiggle her short pink and green hair. "You found yourself a keeper."

Her mom nodded. "Looks like it to me, too. I'm flabbergasted that some of my boys tried to come between these two. After some sleuthing, I'm positive Sky and Marsh aren't in on it. I've also ruled out Lucky and Rance.

"What about Bret?" Angie was dying to know.

"I believe he and Gil are divided on the issue. I can't tell you why I think that. Mother's intuition. But Gil, Cheyenne, Clint and Beau are in up to their necks. I'm disappointed in their behavior and I'm looking for an effective way to handle it, one that won't rip this family right down the middle."

Dallas stiffened. "Is that a possibility?"

"I hope not. We've had disagreements in the family but never anything like this. I'm looking for an intervention that leaves them laughing and sheepish, not angry and nursing a grudge."

"Why those four?" Teresa glanced around the circle. "Why Beau and not Sky? Or Marsh? It's clearly not a matter of the oldest ones being the most overprotective."

"I had a chance to talk privately with Dallas yesterday afternoon," Jess said. "Afterward I started thinking. I came up with a theory, at least about Beau, Clint and Cheyenne. They each jumped into relationships that put the happiness of the family at risk."

"That's for sure." Colleen nodded. "If any one of those hadn't worked out, the fallout around here would've been considerable."

"Not so much with Sky, Marsh and Bret, though," Jess continued. "All relationships involve risk, but theirs were more personal. Doesn't explain Gil, though."

Dallas let out a sigh. "Yes, it does."

What the hell? Angie stared at him. "How?"

"He told me something in confidence. I promised to keep it to myself. But take my word for it, Jess has a good point. These guys each looked disaster in the face and escaped by the skin of their teeth. Now they see us playing with fire and it scares the hell out of them."

"Okay." Her heart softened a little. "That doesn't excuse what they did, though."

"I agree." He met her gaze, his expression gentle. "But a dramatic gotcha moment might not get the results you're looking for."

"Well, damn it."

33

Dallas didn't have much to say during the ride back to Angie's. She and her mom spent the short drive talking about the various suggestions floated during tonight's discussion. Jess had identified the problem, but nobody had come up with a brilliant way to handle it.

Desiree dropped them off with optimistic words and tight hugs. He held hands with Angie as they climbed the steps.

She didn't speak until they were inside. Then she faced him. "You've been very quiet."

"Because what I have to say could only be said to you."

"Your words are lovely but your tone is all doomsday-ish." She took off her jacket and hung it on the coat rack. "Want to get comfy in bed and talk there?"

"It's probably better if we talk here."

She frowned. "Now you're scaring me."

"Sorry." He massaged the back of his tight neck. A doozy of a headache was probably in his future. "There's one part of my conversation with Gil that I can share with you. I've been meaning to, but... no, that's not true. I've been avoiding it."

She shoved her hands in the pockets of her jeans. "Go ahead."

"He mentioned that your mom has stayed friends with the fathers of her kids."

"She has. All except my dad, obviously. But I don't see what—"

"Gil made the point that some women, like your mom for example, can be friends with a man they've had sex with even after they've broken up. Others can't. Like you, for instance."

She blinked. "Sure I could."

"Then you're still friends with some of your exes?"

"No, but they belong to a different time in my life, when I was still searching for what I wanted. So were they. We wouldn't have much in common now that I have more direction."

"What if we broke up? Would you be friends with me?"

"I don't like thinking about that."

"Neither do I, but it's important. Let's say everything works out with your brothers and we get more involved."

"Now you're talkin'."

"We even figure out the two-cabin issue." Might as well throw that into the mix.

"I've wondered about that."

"So have I. But a revolving bookcase beats a pricey rock fireplace any day."

She smiled. "Yeah?"

"That's assuming you were serious about creating one."

"I'll draw up plans tomorrow."

His heart ached with longing. Such a beautiful future, but.... "Now imagine that we hit a roadblock, one we didn't anticipate, and we break up. Cheyenne hasn't rented his place so I move back in."

"I'm not loving this version."

"Me, either. But here's the big question. Please think hard about it. Would you still be friends with me?"

The flash of anxiety in her eyes gave him the answer. Then she lifted her chin. "I'd give it my best shot."

"I believe you'd try. I'm not so sure you'd succeed. Not when I think about your reaction in February."

"But I didn't see that coming. If we had a roadblock, surely I'd notice that big old obstacle ahead of time. It makes a difference if you're somewhat prepared."

"True."

"How about you? Would you be friends with me? Come traipsing over that path to borrow a cup of sugar?"

His gut clenched. "Probably not."

"Then you don't think we could be friends, either."

"It would be tough. On us and everyone else."

"Are you saying my brothers are justified in what they did?"

"Not at all. You have the right to take a risk just like they had that right. If it scares them to think of potential consequences, that's their problem. That said, I—"

"You're not staying tonight, are you?"

He shook his head.

"Oh."

What a sad little sound. Tore him up. He dragged in a breath. "Partly because I'll be working with Cheyenne beginning tomorrow morning. I'll probably be avoiding him as it is. If I spend the whole night with you...."

She laid a hand on his chest. "I get that. I want you to stay, but you're in a tough position for the next three days. Just so you're not breaking up with me."

"I'm not breaking up with you." He surrendered to the deep need to hold her.

She nestled against his chest with a sigh. "Thank you."

"But I need time to think this through more than I have so far. I desperately want your brothers to come around, but what if they don't?"

"They will." She gazed up at him. "They have to."

"Can you guarantee that?"

She gave him a long, sorrowful look. "No."

"And even if they do, there's still the possibility that we might crash and burn."

"Infinitesimal."

"Now I know where you get your big vocabulary."

"You also know that my mom believes in you. In us. Otherwise she wouldn't have told you about M. R. Morrison."

"And I'll cherish that forever." *And you.* The pain in his chest had begun to rival the headache working its way up the back of his skull. "I'd better go before—"

"I seduce you with my wiles?"

"Yes, ma'am." He gave her a quick kiss. "See you on Friday." He backed away, fighting the urge to toss away all his good intentions.

"Want to come here when you get off duty?"

Yes. "Probably shouldn't. Broad daylight and all that. Text me when there's a plan for... whatever your mom comes up with."

"I will." She thrust her hands back into her pockets and stood there, a brave soldier. "Stay safe."

"Always." He was out the front door before he remembered he didn't have wheels. Jogging around the cabin, he connected with the path leading to his place.

Except it wasn't his. He didn't have a lock on any part of this dream. If his presence ever threatened Angie's happiness, he'd put Rowdy Ranch and Wagon Train in the rearview. Simple as that.

34

"I'm bummed." Kendall sipped from her water bottle as she sat next to Angie on the steps of the Emersons' front porch the next morning. They'd finished about a quarter of the screening. "I so wanted to open up a can of whoop-ass on those guys."

"You're welcome to do whatever you want with Cheyenne."

"I know, but I was picturing something more epic landing on his pointy little head. On all of their heads."

"Me, too, but if the goal is to create harmony—"

"I thought the goal was to create revenge."

"I admit that's what I wanted, too. I still feel like smacking them around a little. But if it'll be short-term gain and long-term pain, that makes no sense." She glanced over at her friend. "Dallas wants to move into my house."

Kendall's eyes widened. "He does?"

"Yes, ma'am. I got him with the revolving bookcase plan."

"Put 'er there." Kendall raised her palm.

Angie gave it a good slap. "I know, right? I thought it could be a minor stumbling block, considering he seemed bonkers about Cheyenne's cabin and I wasn't about to leave mine. I've heard of couples who each have a house, but that wouldn't work for me."

"Every so often I wish Cheyenne lived somewhere else."

"Really?"

"Yeah, but it passes, and then I wake up next to him the next morning and love the fact he doesn't have a hidey-hole somewhere. I miss him when he's at the station."

"I miss Dallas already and he's not even living with me yet."

"How do you think those two are getting along today?"

"I'm sure they're both ignoring the elephant in the room. I totally understood why Dallas didn't spend the night with me, but—"

"I think it's kinda sexy that he gave up a bootie call so he could wrap his head around the situation. The man has character."

"He does." Had she picked up on that during the bachelor auction? Doubtful, but how lovely to find out he was beautiful *and* heroic.

"Learning about your mom must have knocked him for a loop. When she told me who she was, I was gobsmacked."

"But here's the takeaway. She trusts him with the information. She trusts him with *me,* and that's what my brothers aren't doing. They're focusing on worst-case scenario instead of best-case."

"Cheyenne would call it *being realistic*. I can just hear him."

"And I call it having your head up your ass."

Kendall laughed. "Can you at least tell them that when the showdown comes? I understand you want this to be a kinder, gentler version of what we had in mind, but I really want to hear you say it to their faces."

"You think I should make a speech?"

"Why not? You did a fabulous job straightening out Clint and Tyra the night of your birthday."

"Huh." She plucked a blade of grass growing near the sidewalk. "That's an idea. I'd assumed Mom would do the talking, but I'm the one most impacted."

"Are you envisioning a Code Red family meeting in the living room on Friday night?"

"Not really...." She wound the blade of grass around her finger. "I know! A family dinner at my place."

"You don't cook."

"But Dallas— wait, I'm not asking him to cook the meal. Besides, I have a special dish in mind."

"Will we fit? There's twenty adults plus Mav and Zach."

"Twenty-one. You forgot Dallas."

"Yikes, I did! I need to adjust my mental count."

"It'll be tight, but if I put both leaves in the table, we can cram everybody in."

"Cozy."

"Exactly what I'm going for. I'll need more chairs and highchairs for Maverick and Zach. I can ask Mom—"

"How about I bring my chairs and little whoozit's highchair?"

"Oh, yeah. I forgot you refinished your old one. But we need two."

"We'll ask Penny if we can borrow theirs for the evening. Let's you and me do this. Your mom can just relax and enjoy it for a change."

"Then will you loan me some dishes and silverware, too?"

"Anything you need. I like this plan."

"I like it, too. I've never had everybody in my house at once. This feels like the perfect time."

"I can't wait to see the look on their faces when you tell them how the cow ate the cabbage."

"Will you be bitterly disappointed if I don't chew them out?"

"You aren't going to? Not even the head-up-the-ass thing?"

"I'm considering a different approach entirely. Like I said, you're welcome to lay into Cheyenne after you get home."

"I reserve that right, but I'll wait to see how your method turns out."

"That's fair." She dropped the blade of grass, took one last swig of water and stood. "We'd better get back to work. Between finishing this porch, grouting the tile in Cheyenne's kitchen and organizing the dinner, we'll have a full week."

"I notice you called it *Cheyenne's kitchen.* Have you already moved Dallas into your place?"

"I did that the minute he told me last night. Cheyenne's going to have to figure out what to do with that cabin because Dallas won't be buying it, after all."

"I love it when you talk like that." Kendall grinned. "You remind me of me."

<u>35</u>

Dallas had accepted Cheyenne's offer of a ride to the station on Tuesday morning. They'd driven in together quite a bit since he'd rented the cabin, switching off between Cheyenne's truck and his.

The ride in hadn't been so bad. They'd talked about the baby due in four months. Or rather, Cheyenne had. Once he got started on the subject, he could go on for quite a while.

Their three-day shift was uneventful, allowing the crew extra time to spit-shine the equipment, execute a few practice drills, work out on the weight benches and play poker. Dallas managed to avoid having any prolonged conversations with Cheyenne.

On the way back Friday morning, though, Cheyenne wanted to discuss the dinner Angie was hosting at her house. "I wonder why she decided to do that? It's not like there's some special occasion we're celebrating or anything."

"Don't ask me, dude." *Please don't ask me. I might let something slip.*

"What's interesting is that she invited you."

"Very interesting."

"Maybe she's decided you're here for the duration and she might as well include you since the whole family's coming. I mean, it would be nice if you could at least be civil to one another, right?"

"That would be nice."

"I'm gonna look at it that way. She feels bad for the way she's been acting toward you since February and wants to let bygones be bygones. I don't think that's the reason for the dinner, but it might be an added benefit, in her mind."

"Anything's possible." Literally. She'd told him that she and Kendall were organizing it and she had high hopes for the outcome. No telling what those two had in store.

He'd offered to cook, but evidently she had that covered — something she was making herself. He'd pressed her for details but she wanted to surprise him. Now there was a sure bet.

Although he wasn't at all surprised she'd taken the bull by the horns and moved the action to her home turf. Or that she'd kept her strategy to herself. The less he knew the better since he'd been interacting with Cheyenne since Tuesday.

"Apparently I'll be eating my lunch on the couch today since we have no kitchen or dining chairs anymore." He didn't sound too upset about it. "I asked Kendall to wait until we got home and we'd help with moving everything. She texted me last night and said they'd taken care of it yesterday."

"Sounds like they're having fun organizing this."

"I get that impression, too."

No, really? What was your first clue? He stared out the window and bit his lip to keep from laughing.

"Kendall loves being part of this big family. I've asked her how many kids she wants, and she keeps dodging the question. I think she has a much larger number in her head than I have in mine, but she doesn't want to freak me out."

"You don't want a big family?"

"It's not that I don't, but you have to be realistic about whether you can afford them. Mom had a lot of kids because she could afford to. You and I won't make that kind of money at the fire department."

"I knew that going in. But it's all I ever wanted to do, other than be a cowboy."

Cheyenne grinned. "And look at that. Now you've got both bases covered. Livin' the dream, buddy."

"That I am." Would tonight's dinner be a dream or a nightmare? He'd put his trust in Angie and hope for the best.

* * *

At five forty-five, he almost blew it. Dressed in his best shirt and a clean pair of jeans, he was out the back door and several yards down the path before he caught himself, doubled back and fetched his truck keys. Good thing none of the McLintocks had driven past and noticed him running around in the forest.

Parking spots were at a premium in front of Angie's house. All were trucks except for Jess's

SUV. She and Beau always took that when Maverick was invited because it had the baby car seat installed.

Speaking of the little tot, she was outside on the porch being passed among folks who had overflowed the house. Cheyenne had her, and then Penny came over and lured her away with a squeaky toy.

Sky stood talking with Molly on the steps. She had her eye on Bret, who'd taken Zack for a walk around the yard. He gripped the toddler's pudgy hand as he executed a bow-legged stagger over the uneven ground.

"Hey, Dallas! Good to see you." Bret's smile radiated the good cheer that was typical of the McLintocks. "Heard you had some bad luck with a water line."

"I did. But Angie and Kendall have finished tiling the floor and Clint will have the cabinets done any day now."

"Yeah, Clint may be sorry he took on that project. Now we all want the drawer arrangement he came up with for yours." He glanced down. "Whoops. Let's not chew on the pinecones, sport." He gently pried it away and substituted a squishy ball he had in his other hand.

"How old is Zach, now?"

"Fifteen months. That means we'll have twenty-one months between Zach and his baby brother."

"Wow, I hadn't heard that news. Congratulations."

Bret lit up. "I think I'm more excited than Molly, and she's over the moon. We can't wait."

Zach turned toward the porch and pointed at Maverick. "Ba-ba, ba-ba."

"He wants to go see Mav." Scooping the little boy up in his arms, Bret started toward the steps. "Now that she's crawling, she's a lot more fun for him to play with."

Dallas followed, climbed the porch steps and responded to the greetings coming his way. He wanted a glimpse of Angie, but this party was a potential minefield. One wrong move on his part might blow up whatever she'd planned.

Maybe staying on the porch was safer. He joined the conversation Sky was having with Molly about which baby car seat was the best. He mostly listened since he had zero to contribute.

Kendall came to the door, flushed and perky, and called everyone inside to eat. The round table where he'd sat with her for that first dinner had become a long oval crammed with chairs. Two highchairs sat nearby.

After much jostling and negotiating, the two couples with babies found their places and positioned the highchairs right behind them. Desiree took one end, flanked by Buck and Marybeth. A large tablecloth covered the wooden surface and a hodgepodge of mismatched dishes and silverware created twenty-one place settings.

No candles tonight. The chandelier was ablaze with lights and although the doors and windows were open in the house, logs crackled in the fireplace.

Angie and Kendall moved around the table offering wine, beer and water. They poured the preferred choice into whatever glass was sitting there.

Three chairs remained empty at the opposite end of where Desiree sat. He, Kendall and Angie were the only ones still standing. Since Cheyenne sat next to the empty chair facing the window, logically Kendall would take that one.

He had no intention of taking the one on the end, so maybe he should go ahead and sit in the one facing the fireplace. But he hesitated.

Clearly this dinner was more choreographed than he'd first thought. Maybe he was supposed to sit next to Cheyenne for some reason. He'd wait to see what Angie had in mind.

Her hair arrangement, the dark curls piled on top of her head, mimicked her mother's updo. Had she ever worn it that way before? Not when he'd been around.

Maybe it was the occasion. Or the hairdo. Or the capable way she tended to her guests. Tonight, for the first time, he saw the strong resemblance to her mom.

Angie was already a force to be reckoned with. By the time she reached Desiree's age, she'd be a legend in her own time, just like her mother. He wanted to be there.

Kendall bustled over and directed him to take the empty seat facing the fire. "What would you like to drink?"

"Beer's fine, thanks."

She poured him a glass and did the same for Angie. Then she filled hers with water. "I'll be across from you and Angie's taking the end. She and

I need to bring in the first course before we sit down."

"Can I help?"

"Thanks for the offer, but we want to. This first course is… symbolic."

"Symbolic?"

"Just go with it. She's got this."

"Okay." He took his seat, which put him next to Molly. Fortunately Cheyenne was deep in a conversation with Penny about baby names, so Dallas chatted with Molly about the B&B she was helping her grandmother develop.

Meanwhile Kendall served finger food to the babies and then helped Angie bring out bowls of soup, setting one on each plate. Smelled delicious.

When all the soup had been delivered, Angie stood behind her chair and cleared her throat. "As you can see, we're starting with chicken soup. And by the way, I made it."

"She's a better cook than she thinks she is," Marybeth said. "She got it on the first try on Tuesday night when I showed her how. This is only her second batch, and I can tell by the way it smells that it's as good or better than mine."

Beau hoisted his glass of beer. "Well done, sis. Now two of us can pass on the family tradition."

"Chicken soup and trust." Sky gave his sister a warm smile. "I've always loved the concept."

Chicken soup and trust? He started to ask, decided against it.

Then Molly did it for him. "What's chicken soup got to do with trust, if I may ask?"

"Everything," Angie said. "For as long as I can remember, whenever we had a family crisis, Marybeth made chicken soup for dinner. She promised us it creates an atmosphere of trust."

"Because it does," Marybeth said.

"Definitely." Jess smiled at Angie. "Beau made it for me when we were trying to navigate the reality of becoming parents. While I didn't trust him instantly the minute I ate some, it was a good start." Then she gave Angie a subtle thumbs-up.

Rance frowned. "Have we got ourselves a crisis? I mean, yeah, a flood happened in what's still technically Cheyenne's kitchen, but that doesn't seem like—"

"Not a crisis, exactly." Angie gazed down the table toward Rance. "Back in February, Dallas and I got crossways. Turns out the broken water line was a blessing for Dallas and me. It allowed us to spend more time together and I've discovered he's a great guy."

Across the table, Cheyenne's eyebrows shot up. He looked over at Dallas, who gave him a shrug.

"I could have told you that, sis." Lucky spoke up from his spot next to Rance. "He comes in the bookstore all the time. I wondered why you didn't like him. I mean, he loves books. What more do you need to know? I'm glad he moved here."

Totally confused, Dallas murmured a quick *thanks.* Where was Angie going with this? Cheyenne's eyebrows had lowered into a frown. He murmured something to Kendall, who patted his arm.

"Well, I for one am happy as a speckled pup that you two are speaking again." Beau's smile brimmed with good will.

"It goes a little deeper than that." Glancing over at Dallas, Angie reached over and squeezed his shoulder.

His breath caught. What was she up to?

Then she gave him a wink.

A *wink?* Holy hell. He took a sip of beer to calm his nerves.

"I've invited him to move in with me."

He spewed his beer.

"Sorry, sweetheart." She handed him a napkin. "I knew if I told you that was the reason for arranging this dinner, you'd try to talk me out of it."

No shit. He mopped his face and gave her a *what-the-hell* glance.

She laid her hand on his shoulder again as her gaze circled the table. "Dallas is more low-key than I am, which is one of the many things that makes us a perfect match. I think he would have preferred talking to you individually, or at least in smaller groups. But I know you all think the world of him, and you also trust my good judgment, so why waste time slow-playing it?"

Desiree left her chair and raised her glass. "I'm thrilled for you and Dallas. I've never seen you looking so happy. Here's to Angie and Dallas!"

Dallas stood, picked up his glass and dared to look at Cheyenne. His friend rose to his feet, his gaze on Dallas as he picked up his beer. Would he throw it across the table?

Nope. Damned if a sheepish grin didn't spread across his handsome mug as he lifted his beer.

By then everyone was standing, including the other three members of that interfering posse. Each one of them mirrored Cheyenne's expression. Was there a shimmer of relief in their eyes?

He took a breath. "Angie's right. I would have tried to talk her out of this event, but as usual, her instincts were on target. This is perfect." He turned to her, meeting her sparkling gaze. "Thank you." Touching his glass to hers, he took a sip. Then he leaned over and gave her a gentle kiss as everyone cheered and glasses clinked.

As he ended the brief kiss, he muttered. "Later."

"You bet."

<u>36</u>

Angie wasn't great at spooning up soup left-handed, but she managed. Dallas had claimed her right hand under the table. She wasn't about to break that connection for some silly thing like eating soup. It was damn tasty soup though.

So was the rest of the meal. She and Kendall had spent the day on it, with Kendall providing the know-how and Angie contributing sweat equity.

Talk flowed freely around the table in a way that it hadn't for the past three months. Her four misbehaving brothers laughed more readily and smiled more often. They'd thought they were saving her and instead she'd saved them.

Would they ever confess what they'd done? Maybe not. And that was okay. They got the message. She wasn't little Angie anymore and she would choose her own path, thank you very much.

The path ahead sure looked inviting, especially every time Dallas gave her hand a squeeze and she gazed into his sexy brown eyes. Made her stomach flutter. Tonight would be one for the record books.

Often after a meal, the family would clear the table and break out the poker chips. Not tonight. Everyone pitched in to load the dishwasher but then the goodbyes started, with plenty of hugs and praise for the fabulous food.

Kendall and Cheyenne were the last to leave. Kendall gave Dallas a hug.

Then Cheyenne held out his hand, his gaze steady. "Hey, buddy. You've got yourself a gem."

"I know."

Angie held her breath. Cheyenne was the brother who might feel the most betrayed by tonight's events.

He gripped Dallas's hand a moment longer. "You two will be great together." He smiled and let go. "I'm happy for you."

Okay, then. She relaxed.

"Thanks, Cheyenne." Dallas hesitated. "You're not ticked off about the cabin?"

"Hell, no. I gave you the friends and family rate. I'll rent it to somebody I don't care about and charge them an arm and a leg. Makes more sense than selling since it provides passive income."

That made her chuckle. "I'll bet Kendall taught you that."

"She did. I'm learning about investments, too." He held Angie's gaze. "Kendall's always teaching me something."

"I believe it."

"So are you." He opened his arms. "Bring it in, sis." He gave her a tight hug, pressing his cheek to hers. "I'm sorry," he murmured.

Clearly his soft confession was meant for her ears only. She hugged him harder, tears pushing at the backs of her eyes. "I forgive you."

"Thanks. Love you, sis."

"Love you, too."

He backed away. Her rugged, self-reliant brother was misty-eyed.

Kendall moved in and gave her a bear hug. "You did great."

"*We* did great." She lowered her voice. "He said sorry. Be nice."

"Okay."

After they left, Dallas turned to her. "Did I hear you tell Kendall that he apologized?"

She nodded, her throat tight. "I pretended it didn't matter if he did or not, but—"

"It does." He folded her in his arms. "It matters to me, too. It wasn't a proud moment for any of them, but they saw the light." He met her gaze. "Thanks to you. You were amazing."

She basked in the warmth in his eyes. "I pulled a fast one on you, though."

"You had to. By not telling me your plan, you made it obvious that announcement was not my idea. You saved my ass along with theirs."

"I didn't see you take a mouthful of beer, though. I was looking at everybody else. Sorry about that."

"It was the perfect touch. They knew for sure I was clueless. By the way, how did you come up with this concept?"

"Kendall thought I should make a speech at a family meeting at the ranch house, although she wanted me to call them out. At some point I realized how awful that would be. So I found another way."

"A brilliant way. You accomplished exactly what your mom hoped for."

"I kind of pinned you to the wall with my announcement, though."

"Did you?"

"You said you'd choose my place over yours, but you didn't say you were ready to—"

"Are you kidding? I've been ready to be with you for a damn year. Let's do it. Can't be too soon for me."

"Are you saying you want to load up your truck tonight?"

He smiled. "Maybe not tonight. Tomorrow works. I have other plans for tonight."

She snuggled closer. "Sounds good to me. The kitchen's clean enough for now. Wanna head back to—"

"Not yet."

"Why not?"

"Before I kiss you again, before I lose myself in that delicious body of yours, I have something to say."

Her heart pounded faster. Unless she was sadly mistaken, he was about to tell her something Very Important. "I'm listening."

"I've been crazy about you ever since I moved out here, and every day I kept hoping—"

"Hang on. I'm starting to hyperventilate." She dragged in a breath.

"Yeah, me, too." He swallowed. "I've never said something like this."

"Me, either."

"You have something to say, too?"

She nodded.

"Maybe I should cut to the chase."

"Please. Before we both pass out."

Holding her gaze, he took a ragged breath. "I love you, Angie. I love you so much, and I—"

"I love you, too! And I know we said we weren't in any hurry, but—"

"I'm in a hurry."

Her heart pounded so hard she grew dizzy. "Me, too. I think we should—"

"Get married."

"Yes, yes, yes, y—"

His kiss swallowed the last *yes*, but the word kept dancing in her head, in her heart, in her soul. When it came to Dallas, it was her favorite word of all.

* * * * *

His brother's wedding pushes Gil McLintock
into forced proximity with his disastrous first-
time lover, Faye Bradley, in
CRAVING THE COWBOY'S KISS, book seven in
the Rowdy Ranch series!

* * * * *

New York Times bestselling author Vicki Lewis Thompson's love affair with cowboys started with the Lone Ranger, continued through Maverick, and took a turn south of the border with Zorro. She views cowboys as the Western version of knights in shining armor, rugged men who value honor, honesty and hard work. Fortunately for her, she lives in the Arizona desert, where broad-shouldered, lean-hipped cowboys abound. Blessed with such an abundance of inspiration, she only hopes that she can do them justice.

For more information about this prolific author, visit her website and sign up for her newsletter. She loves connecting with readers.

VickiLewisThompson.com

Ingram Content Group UK Ltd.
Milton Keynes UK
UKHW010647260723
425809UK00004B/189